Opposites attracte

Skyler closed her eyes a
the headrest. Images of
her mind. She didn't have to admit it to her
matchmaking friends, but he was pretty dang hot.
Tall, with strong, wide shoulders, a naughty smile
and dark hair that was made for a woman's hands
to run through.

Logan Bradshaw was only here visiting and would
be gone soon. But India had thought Liam was
going to be gone in a matter of days, too. Instead,
he'd moved his business from Fort Worth to Blue
Falls and proposed marriage.

Skyler laughed under her breath before she
caught herself.

"What?" Elissa asked as she put the SUV in Drive.

"Nothing." But as she stared out the window at
the coming twilight, Skyler almost laughed again
at the idea of Logan asking anyone to marry him,
especially someone as opposite to him as her.

Dear Reader,

It's time to return to the lovely tourist town of Blue Falls, Texas, to find out which unsuspecting local resident is in the sights of matchmaker Verona Charles. Last time around, it was boutique owner India Pike in *Her Perfect Cowboy,* and she certainly didn't mind finding her true love in Liam Parrish. And with so many yummy cowboys in town, it would be a shame not to find the perfect woman for at least one of them.

So when Verona meets bull rider Logan Bradshaw, she immediately knows he'd be perfect for one of India's best friends, Skyler Harrington. Only one problem— Skyler, who owns the Wildflower Inn and likes things just so, can't imagine a worse match for herself. There's a little too much of the rootless wanderlust that she'd grown up seeing in her father. But even though she knows Logan isn't the guy for her, she can't deny the incredible physical attraction between them. And as she gets to know him, she begins to wonder if he can change and become someone she could love and be loved by.

At first, Logan actually agrees with Skyler that he's not a settling-down sort of guy. But when a night of passion leads to Skyler getting pregnant, he begins to wonder if it's time to stop his wandering ways and be a responsible father. As he gets to know Skyler better, he realizes the baby isn't the only reason he's thinking Blue Falls just might be his new home.

Happy reading,

Trish

HAVING THE COWBOY'S BABY

—

TRISH MILBURN

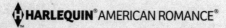

HARLEQUIN® AMERICAN ROMANCE®

Recycling programs
for this product may
not exist in your area.

ISBN-13: 978-0-373-75472-4

HAVING THE COWBOY'S BABY

Printed in U.S.A.

ABOUT THE AUTHOR

Trish Milburn writes contemporary romance for Harlequin American Romance and paranormal romance for Harlequin Nocturne. She's a two-time Golden Heart award winner, a fan of walks in the woods and road trips, and is a big geek girl, including being a dedicated Whovian and Browncoat. And from her earliest memories, she's been a fan of Westerns, be they historical or contemporary. There's nothing quite like a cowboy hero.

Books by Trish Milburn

HARLEQUIN AMERICAN ROMANCE

*The Teagues of Texas
**Blue Falls, Texas

To my mom. Even though she was never able to read my books, she did love a good cowboy story. We watched many a Western together when I was a kid, and she still watched *Bonanza, The Big Valley* and *Dr. Quinn, Medicine Woman* every day until her passing. I miss you, Mom, and I hope you're watching lots of Westerns in Heaven. Maybe you're even riding a horse of your own.

Chapter One

Skyler Harrington smoothed her new cream-colored pencil skirt as she took her seat at the corner table at La Cantina. She pointed at the enormous platter of nachos that sat on the table between her and her two best friends, India Pike and Elissa Mason. Elissa was in the midst of grabbing a nacho laden with beef, sour cream and gooey cheese.

"Glad to see you all waited for me," Skyler said.

India nodded toward Elissa, who was now stuffing said nacho into her mouth. "She threatened to start gnawing on her arm if we didn't get something to eat pronto."

"What?" Elissa said around her food. "I was starving. You try unloading a truckload of shrubbery and see if you're not hungry."

She had a point. While each of them owned her own business, Elissa's plant nursery required more physical labor than India's clothing boutique or Skyler's inn.

"Plus," Elissa said as she pointed another nacho at Skyler, "you were late."

Skyler's forehead scrunched as she reached for her phone to check the time. It was exactly one minute after six, and she knew she'd been at the restaurant more than a minute already.

Elissa laughed.

Skyler lifted her narrowed gaze to her friend, who was teasing her yet again about her preference for being places on time, or better yet, early. "I don't know why I'm friends with you."

Elissa smiled. "Because I'm so lovable."

"That's debatable."

"You let her get you every time," India said.

"One of these days maybe I'll figure out what she finds so funny about my punctuality."

"You call it punctuality, I call it inability to go with the flow," Elissa said.

"I can go with the flow." It made her twitchy, but she could do it. "I'm not as big of a stick in the mud as you seem to think."

"Oh, really? When was the last time you really let go and didn't plan your day out to within an inch of its life?"

Skyler opened her mouth but then couldn't think of an answer that wouldn't prove Elissa's point. "I have a lot of responsibilities, people depending on me."

"And we don't?"

"Hey, I'm not that different from India." At least India before Liam Parrish strode into town with his cowboy boots, a Stetson and two very long legs. India's well-ordered life had gone topsy-turvy in two seconds flat. Not that Skyler blamed her. Liam wasn't just good-looking. He also was a really good guy and would become the closest thing Skyler had to a brother when he and India got married in a few weeks.

Skyler grabbed a nacho and scraped most of the toppings off of it back onto the platter.

"You're getting rid of all the good stuff," Elissa said.

"A little goes a long way. Now I'll actually be able to taste the chip."

Elissa rolled her eyes. "Can't even eat a nacho without overthinking it."

"I'll remind you of that when your arteries get clogged with cheese."

Elissa just smiled, stuffed another nacho in her mouth and mmmed her taste buds' appreciation.

Skyler didn't know whether she wanted to throw something at Elissa or give in and eat a heaping nacho herself.

After the waitress took their orders, Skyler turned her attention to India before Elissa had the chance to start bugging the living daylights out of her again.

"So how are the final plans for the wedding going? Is there anything else you need me to do?"

India's eyes lit up at the mention of her upcoming nuptials, causing Skyler's heart to warm. After everything she'd been through, India deserved to be happy.

"I don't think so. You've done so much already, both of you."

"It's not every day your best friend gets married to the hottest guy in town," Elissa said.

On that point, Elissa and Skyler could agree.

"I wish it was tomorrow," India said.

Skyler smiled. "That anxious to make an honest man out of Liam?"

India laughed. "If there was more to do between now and then, I'd be fine. But the waiting might kill me. You know what would really help?"

"What?"

"Another project."

India and Elissa exchanged a look that made Skyler nervous. "Why do I feel like I've missed something really important?"

"Your thirtieth birthday is two days away and we haven't planned what we're going to do," India said. "That would keep my mind occupied."

"It doesn't take that long to look up movie times in Austin," Skyler said.

India raised an eyebrow. "I think the occasion calls for more than a movie."

"I happen to quite like watching Jeremy Renner and his awesome arms."

"Well, I can't argue with you there," Elissa said. "But India's right. We can do a movie anytime. I was thinking of something more exciting."

"Of course you were."

Elissa sighed and leaned back in her chair. She glanced at India. "I told you she wouldn't be up for anything interesting."

The sudden overwhelming urge to prove her friend wrong rose up in Skyler. "Fine. You know what? You all can plan whatever you want, and I'll do it."

Elissa barked out a disbelieving laugh. "Yeah, right."

"Really. I'll let you plan the whole thing." The moment the words were out of her mouth, she wanted to call them back and pretend they were never uttered. But if she backed out now, she would never, ever hear the end of it. Blast Elissa for causing her emotions to override her common sense.

The smile that spread across Elissa's face told Skyler she'd just made perhaps the biggest mistake of her life.

"Is it Christmas?" Elissa asked. "Because it feels like Christmas."

"Don't gloat," India said, but she looked like she was having a hard time keeping from smiling, too.

Skyler really knew she was in trouble when their food arrived and Elissa didn't immediately attack her quesadillas. Instead, she was scrolling through something on her phone.

Skyler picked up her fork and stirred the contents of her taco salad. "You know it's rude to have your face buried in your phone when you're with other people, right?"

"This is important business."

"A mulch emergency?"

"I'll have you know I'm doing research, with a little help from Verona."

Skyler stopped with her fork halfway to her mouth, warning bells clanging in her head. "Verona?"

"Yes, you know, my aunt."

Skyler narrowed her eyes. "I don't trust you or your aunt."

"Why not? You have to admit she got it right with India and Liam."

"Yes, but that doesn't mean I want her anywhere near my personal life."

"Verona does more than matchmake, you know."

"What, she's giving you tourist suggestions? I've lived in Texas my whole life. Pretty sure there aren't that many places of interest I've not been to."

Elissa waved off her concern. "Hush. Eat your salad."

Knowing that short of snatching Elissa's phone from her there was nothing she could do, Skyler refocused her attention on her meal. Her stomach growled in response. She'd been so busy during the day that she hadn't taken time for a real lunch, nothing beyond the bag of apple slices she'd snagged from her fridge on the way out of her apartment that morning.

Sure, since her apartment was located at the inn, she could have gone to get something else to eat or ordered something from the kitchen, but a staff meeting had led to several phone calls, which had flowed into going over a contract for fresh produce. The next thing she knew, it was time to leave to meet her friends for dinner.

When Elissa set down her phone, the satisfied smile on her face didn't bode well for Skyler.

"What do you have up your sleeve?"

"Who, me?"

Skyler slowly rested her fork on top of what was left of her salad. "You shouldn't try to sound innocent. You're not very good at it."

Elissa shrugged. "Who wants to be innocent anyway when there's so much fun to be had?"

"I'm afraid to ask what kind of 'fun' you have in mind."

"I wouldn't tell you, anyway."

"Um, it's *my* birthday."

Elissa finally looked up after she took a bite of her dinner and swallowed. "And birthdays include surprises."

"You know I'm not a fan of surprises." They'd rarely turned out well in her experience.

Surprise! Your dad's gone to Alaska to fish.

Surprise! He's back again with no warning and who knows for how long.

Surprise! Your mom had a heart attack and died.

"You'll like this one."

Skyler doubted that and considered booking a last-minute vacation for one to the Caribbean.

"And no, we're not letting you weasel out of this, so stop trying to concoct a way to do just that." Elissa gestured toward Skyler's head as if she knew exactly what she was thinking. She probably did.

"Sometimes it's highly annoying that you know me so well."

As Elissa and India laughed, Skyler felt like kicking herself all the way to El Paso and back for giving them just enough rope to hang her with.

Skyler was on the verge of asking Elissa again where the devil they were going when she spotted a sign on the side of the road just as Elissa started to slow down. Hill Country Adventure Sports.

"Please tell me this isn't our final destination, that you're delivering plants or something."

Elissa glanced at her from the driver's seat of the SUV. "Nope, this is the place."

Skyler turned halfway to look at India and Verona in the back. "Tell me she's kidding."

India shook her head. "It'll be fun."

Skyler looked from one friend to the other, wondering if they'd been body snatched. Because the Elissa and India she knew wouldn't go this far. "Are you smoking crack? There is no way I'm jumping out of a perfectly good airplane."

"Yes, you are," Elissa said as if Skyler was being silly. "You only live once."

"Yeah, and I'd like to live beyond today, thank you very much."

"They're not going to push you out without a parachute, dear," Verona said.

"It's tandem diving," India added. "You jump with an experienced diver who is trained."

Elissa took her hand off the steering wheel long enough to wave away Skyler's concern. "They've done this a million times."

"All it takes is one time when it doesn't go as planned."

Elissa shook her head as she parked next to a long building that contained an office and several hangar bays for small planes. "I knew you were a compulsive planner, but I didn't know you were a chicken."

"I'm not. I'm sane."

Ignoring her protests, everyone else got out of the car and headed toward the office. She wondered what they'd do if she flatly refused to budge. It was her birthday, damn it. She ought to be able to choose what she wanted to do and not do. And skydiving was way up on the "not do" list.

But the longer she sat in the SUV, the more fidgety she grew. Hurtling through thin air was definitely not on her bucket list, but she didn't like that the mere thought of jumping could get the better of her either. She wanted to believe she could do anything even if she chose not to, but she'd given her friends permission to take this decision out of her hands. Big mistake, but one she was going to have to swallow.

She cursed under her breath as she opened the door, shut it none too gently and closed the distance between her and her so-called friends.

"I'm so sorry," said Jesse Bradshaw as she got close enough to hear him speaking to Elissa, India and Verona. "I must have caught a stomach bug. I can't dive today."

Oh, hallelujah, birthday wishes were granted!

"That's too bad," India said.

"Man, we'll never get her out here again," Elissa said before she noticed Skyler.

Something was off about her friends' responses to the news that Jesse was sick, but she couldn't put her finger on it.

"She can still go up. My cousin will just be the diver, not me."

Skyler fought the urge to run all the way back to Blue Falls. "I didn't know you had a cousin, Jesse." She scanned the area but saw no one else but the pilot, next to a small red-and-white plane on the tarmac, and the jet-fuel delivery guy.

"Yeah, he's in town visiting. I just called him a few minutes ago. He's on his way. He wasn't expecting to have to dive today."

"Oh, I don't want to put anyone to any trouble," Skyler said.

"It's no trouble."

The sound of a pickup heading toward them on the gravel entrance road drew everyone's attention.

"That's him now," Jesse said.

A red pickup truck that looked like it had seen better days, better decades, rolled to a stop next to Elissa's SUV, leaving a cloud of gravel dust in its wake.

When the driver stepped out of the truck and strode toward them, Skyler thought there had to be some mistake. This guy looked about as much like a skydiver as Verona did. With worn jeans, scuffed boots and a dark brown cowboy hat, he would look more at home on a cattle drive. When he nodded at her friends and said, "Hello again," Skyler definitely knew something was up.

"This is all a big joke, isn't it? I'm being punked."

"Well, that's not usually the reaction I get from the ladies," the guy said as he stopped a couple of feet away, his lips stretching into a mischievous smile.

Skyler gave him a raised-eyebrow look before shifting her attention to the other three women. "Seriously, what is going on?"

Before they could answer, the guy laughed. "Don't worry, I don't dive in the boots."

She glanced at him. "Just the hat?"

"Nah. I'd lose it as soon as we jumped."

"Lucky for you, there won't be any jumping today."

"But we've already paid for it," India said.

"Then I suggest you get your money back." When Skyler glanced at Jesse, he had an apologetic look on his face.

"I'm sorry, but there's a no-refund policy on the deposit unless canceled by inclement weather," he said.

Skyler sighed heavily as she looked up into the bright blue sky devoid of clouds. You couldn't ask for a more beautiful day, unless, of course, you were hoping to avoid plummeting to your death.

"Come on, Jesse," the still-nameless cousin said. "You can allow the refund."

Surprised by his siding with her, Skyler met his eyes. "Thank you."

"Ah, come on," Elissa said. "Everyone I know who has done this has loved it. Heck, Jesse jumped with McKenna Parks's eighty-seven-year-old grandpa last week, and the old guy is ready to go again. Right, Jesse?"

Jesse, to his credit, looked uncomfortable being put in the middle of their disagreement. But he nodded. "He wanted to go back up as soon as we hit the ground."

She knew Elissa was daring her, effectively taking away any nonchicken way of backing out of the dive. Skyler shifted her eyes to Jesse's cousin. "Just how many dives have you done?"

He smiled. "Enough."

For a moment she let herself appreciate how that smile only added to how good-looking he was. Good-looking, ha! The man was three-alarm fire, drop-dead gorgeous.

She snatched her gaze away from his. She did not need to be thinking about dropping dead, or about how Mr. No Name looked good enough to lick up one side and down the other. Her face flamed, and for once she was glad to have fair skin and red hair. It made blaming the flush on the sun totally believable.

The guy leaned close and used a faux whisper to say, "Don't worry, beautiful. I promise you're safe with me."

She wondered how many times he'd used that line. Because the cowboy was a flirt and most likely a class A player.

The longer she stood there with everyone looking at her, the more she had to fight fidgeting. She closed her eyes for a moment and pulled together all the fragments of her courage. "Fine, I'll do it."

It was smart to face your fears, right? At the very least, she could stick her tongue out at Elissa after it was over.

"Just give me a few minutes to suit up, and I'll give you the ride of your life," her dive partner said.

Skyler glanced at him in time to see him wink. She'd never admit it out loud, but she felt that wink all the way to her toes. She shook her head and rolled her eyes as he walked away. When Jesse followed him, Skyler spun toward her friends.

"So, what do you think?" Verona asked.

"What do I—? This isn't one of your matchmaking schemes, is it?"

Verona's eyes widened. "How could it be? We didn't find out about Jesse being sick until we got here."

Skyler wasn't buying it. She wasn't exactly sure what was going on, but she got the distinct feeling it was more than it appeared on the surface.

"For the record, I know you all are up to something."

"But you're going through with the dive, right?" India asked.

"Do I have a choice?"

"No," Elissa said with a boatload more cheer in her voice than the occasion called for. "We're giving you the experience of a lifetime."

"I could have handled canoeing, maybe a wad of dollar bills and a strip club, but no, you all give me the skydiving cowboy and a potential coronary."

"You're in perfect health," India said.

"And that skydiving cowboy is yum-my," Elissa added.

"I don't care what he looks like as long as he keeps me from going splat against the ground. And just so you know, if I die, I'm coming back and haunting all of you at the most inconvenient times."

When skydiving cowboy came back outside, followed by his cousin, he looked more skydiver than cowboy. With the Stetson gone, she was able to see more of his short dark hair, angular jaw and dark eyes. If she'd met him somewhere else under different circumstances, he would have definitely caught her eye.

What was she doing? She had to concentrate on surviving the next hour, not lusting over this guy who probably got laid more than carpet. Reluctantly, she followed him toward the plane, her stomach churning.

"So what did they convince you to do?" she asked.

He glanced at her, genuine confusion in his expression. "Jump out of an airplane?"

She stopped walking halfway to the plane. "You met them before, right?"

"Yeah, yesterday at the café. Why?"

Skyler shook her head. "Never mind." She glanced back in time to see her friends smiling ear to ear. "I am going to kill them." She didn't realize she'd said the words loud enough for anyone to hear until her diving partner laughed.

"Killing's over too quickly," he said. "Payback's better."

"You know, you're right. And I can be very creative."

His mouth quirked up at one edge. "That right?"

The innuendo caused her skin to tingle all over, and that only made her more determined to find the perfect payback for her friends. But first she evidently had to throw common sense to the wind and take a literal leap of faith.

The next few minutes went by in a blur as they boarded the plane, the pilot took off and they geared up for the dive. As they approached the designated point for the jump, Skyler felt as though she might throw up.

"It's okay. Once you're out there flying, you'll forget all about the nerves." He sounded so casual and relaxed, as if hurling one's self from an airplane was no big deal.

"Somehow I doubt that."

"Trust me."

"Trust you? I don't even know your name."

"Tell me yours and I'll tell you mine," he said, mischief in his voice.

"You have a line for everything, don't you?"

"Yep."

"Well, at least your honesty is refreshing." She glanced toward where another guy slid the side door open to reveal nothing but sky. She swallowed hard as cowboy dude moved up behind her and did whatever it was he had to do to connect their gear together.

"Logan Bradshaw," he said, his voice rumbling in her ear.

"What?"

"My name, Logan Bradshaw."

"Oh. Skyler Harrington."

Her heart leaped into her throat as he urged her toward the open doorway.

"Ten seconds," the other guy said.

Oh, Lord.

"Well, Skyler Harrington, you and I are going to go out after this is over," Logan said.

And then he pushed her out the door, and she greeted her birthday with a scream.

Chapter Two

At some point Skyler stopped screaming and realized that the sight before her was nothing short of awe-inspiring. All her fear wasn't gone, maybe just on hold as she scanned the world spread out below her.

"Beautiful, isn't it?" Logan said over the sound of the wind rushing past her ears.

All she could do was nod as she picked out familiar landmarks, the cluster of buildings that made up Blue Falls, the water tower painted with bluebonnets and the words *Blue Falls, Wildflower Capital of Texas*.

Despite her fear, an incredible sense of freedom washed over her. As her eyes took in the distant hills, the spots of green vegetation the drought hadn't yet battered into submission and the glittering surface of the lake, she was stunned by a world she took for granted every day. Up here there was no responsibility, no pressure, no expectations. Hopefully Logan had all of those under control. It was a bit like an out-of-body experience, an away-from-earth experience that was nothing like being in an airplane.

"I'm going to pull the parachute," Logan said, reminding her that she was, in fact, plummeting toward earth.

She cried out when the parachute deployed, jerking against her.

"It's okay. Look up."

After she managed to get her heart rate to slow a fraction, she looked up and saw the width of the white parachute catching air and slowing their descent. That's when she remembered what Logan said right before he pushed her out of the plane. He probably thought he was cute, that she would melt at his interest. Well, all she was interested in from Logan Bradshaw was him getting her safely to the ground.

Gradually, the world below grew in size until it no longer resembled a collection of miniatures. Logan guided their parachute toward an area devoid of trees and other obstacles. Their speed seemed to increase the closer they got to the ground, and Skyler tensed.

"Relax," he said.

"Easy for you to say."

"This isn't my first time."

Now, why did she immediately imagine him in bed when he said that? Good grief, she didn't even like him. She'd never been one to go for guys who were so full of themselves that there was no room for anyone else.

Maybe if he got a personality transplant…

She spotted India, Elissa and Verona in the distance, and she hated the idea of having to admit that she'd liked the dive despite the pulse-racing fear of a deadly altercation with gravity.

"Here we go," Logan said as the ground raced up to meet them.

Before she could take another breath, her feet touched terra firma.

"See, all in one piece," Logan said, laughter in his way too sexy voice.

"Wonders never cease." She should really thank him. He had, after all, kept her safe while giving her an experience like none she'd ever imagined. But he was just so cocky about it.

And damned if a little sliver of her didn't find that attractive. She had to get away from him as soon as possible.

"How was it?" Elissa asked as she and the others hurried toward where Logan was unhooking Skyler from her gear.

"It was okay."

Logan snorted.

Skyler looked at him, not even trying to hide her annoyance. "What was that for?"

He met her gaze and refused to look away. "You enjoyed it."

"How do you know that? You couldn't even see my face."

"I can tell when someone is enjoying herself."

There it was again, enough innuendo to make her blush.

"Your face is all red," Elissa said, teasing.

Skyler jerked her gaze away from Logan and focused on her friend. "Well, I didn't put on SPF 8 billion today. I wasn't expecting to be so danged close to the sun."

"I saw the Ice Cream Hut is still down by the lake," Logan said. "Not a bad choice for a first date, don't you think?"

"Date?" Verona's eyes widened with totally uncontained glee.

"Yeah, the deal was that I get birthday girl safely to the ground, she goes out with me."

Skyler's mouth dropped open as she spun toward Logan, her hands on her hips. "I did not agree to that. You made your pronouncement a breath before you shoved me out of a plane. I don't know you from Adam."

"Isn't that what dates are for, getting to know each other?"

"Sounds like a good idea to me," Elissa said.

"There will be no date. It's my birthday, so here's a crazy thought. How about I pick how I spend the rest of the day and who I spend it with?" She eyed the other women. "And I'm not sure any of you are on that list."

With that, she stalked toward Elissa's SUV. If she didn't

fear her skin being burned to a crisp by the time she got back to Blue Falls, she'd walk.

Not that she had any confidence that walking those miles was going to do anything to erase cocky, full-of-himself... sexy Logan Bradshaw from her mind. Yet another reason her friends deserved one whale of a payback.

"I'M SORRY she's so cranky." Verona shook her head as she glanced at Skyler's retreating form.

"No worries." He watched as Skyler stalked away, her jeans showing off her shapely backside. "She'll come around."

He didn't think he was the world's best catch or anything, but he liked to have a good time. And if anyone was in dire need of a good time, it was uptight Skyler Harrington. It had taken him only one look at the gorgeous redhead to know he wanted to be the man to get her to loosen up a little and enjoy herself.

"Maybe we can help a little bit with that," said the taller, dark-haired woman, the one who seemed to be more prone to teasing Skyler. Elissa, that was her name. "We're having a surprise party at the music hall tonight. You should come."

"Sure, sounds like fun." He eyed the SUV where Skyler now sat staring out the windshield instead of in his direction. Even from this distance, he could tell she was as rigid as a telephone pole.

When all the women had left, he finished gathering the gear and tossed it into the back of Jesse's pickup truck. He slipped into the passenger seat.

"Feeling better, cuz?"

Jesse glanced over at Logan's knowing tone. "Listen, you don't say no to Verona Charles. Not if you don't want her matchmaking mojo pointed in your direction."

"So that's what this is all about? Setting me up with Skyler? Why all the secrecy? When have you known me to not want to go out with a beautiful woman?"

"That was their crazy idea, not mine. After you left the café, Verona asked a lot of questions about you. I guess you passed her test, because that's when she started talking about setting up a way for you two to meet without Skyler getting wind of it."

"Because she wouldn't have gone along with it."

"Bingo. She's not your normal type."

Logan stretched his arm out along the back of the truck's bench seat and stared at his cousin. "And what type is that?"

"Just looking for a good time."

"Part of me thinks I ought to be offended."

Jesse laughed.

The last thing Logan needed was to get involved with a woman who was more the settling-down type. His skin itched just thinking about it.

"So, what are you doing the rest of the day?" Jesse asked as he parked next to Logan's old truck.

"Going to check out the arena at the fairgrounds, get the lay of the land."

They got out of Jesse's truck and stopped at the back of Logan's.

"You still enjoying riding?"

"Nothing like it." Sitting astride a bucking bull was so far from his go-nowhere, do-nothing childhood existence that he'd latched on to it the first chance he'd gotten. He dreaded the day when his body prevented him from doing it anymore. Riding bulls was kind of like skydiving—exciting, pushing the edge. They both gave him that sense of freedom he craved as much as air and water.

"Adrenaline junkie-ism must run in the family."

Logan snorted. "Maybe yours."

"Maybe just our generation."

Logan let the conversation drop, even though he could have easily pointed out that his siblings seemed content to follow in their parents' unadventurous footsteps. That Jesse's dad had shown the first daredevil tendencies when he'd left North Dakota and joined the air force. And then instead of coming back after his stint was over, he'd gone off to Texas and started flying small planes for executives and vintage planes for air shows. Of the four Bradshaw kids in the older generation, Uncle James was the only one who "got away." He still hadn't heard the end of it from the rest of the family in North Dakota.

Just as Logan still heard about his own defection every time he called home. He loved his parents, but that conversation got really damned old.

He shook his head to clear the unwanted memories. "Well, I'll catch you later."

"I'll see you at the rodeo if not before then."

Logan thought about inviting Jesse to Skyler's shindig at the music hall, but he kept quiet. As out of character as it might be, he was considering not going. Sure, he'd taken a doozy of a fall off a bull the previous weekend, but he didn't think he'd hit his head so hard that he was suddenly avoiding beautiful women. But he got the distinct impression that Skyler Harrington wasn't just any beautiful woman.

She was way too much trouble personified. Even if she was hot as a firecracker.

"Now, see, we're not all bad," Elissa said as she walked out of the movie theater next to Skyler and India.

Skyler eyed Elissa as her friend shifted to walking backward in front of her. "Yes, this is more of what I had in mind in the first place." A giant movie screen with Jeremy Renner's fabulous arms on full display and a tub of buttery popcorn—what wasn't to like?

"Although why you'd prefer your movie boyfriend over an actual living, breathing hottie, I have no idea." Elissa shrugged.

"Maybe because my 'movie boyfriend' doesn't think he's God's gift to women."

"Aw, come on, what's wrong with a little flirting?"

Skyler reached the SUV and stood with her arms crossed. "What was it India said when you were pushing her toward Liam so hard? Oh, yeah. 'Then you go out with him.'"

"I think India's probably glad that I didn't take her suggestion."

"Sorry, but she's right about that," India said.

Elissa hit the key fob to unlock the doors, and Skyler chose to sit in the back this time. She eyed Elissa when her friend slid into the driver's seat.

"You and Verona aren't going to be satisfied until you've paired up everyone in Blue Falls, are you?"

"Once again, the surefire way to keep Verona pointed away from me and my personal life is to shift her in other directions."

"Thanks for throwing me under the bus." Skyler met India's eyes when India glanced into the back. "Tell me again why we're friends with her."

"Half price on landscaping supplies?"

"Drat. I guess I have to keep her."

All three of them ended up laughing. There was no sense in staying irritated with her two best friends in the world. After all, it wasn't as if she had to worry about Logan Bradshaw anymore. Being a lifelong resident of Blue Falls meant she knew everyone who lived in the area, and Logan didn't. He was only here visiting his cousin and would be gone soon.

But India had thought Liam was going to be gone in a matter of days, too. Instead, he'd moved his business from Fort Worth to Blue Falls and proposed marriage.

Skyler laughed under her breath before she caught herself.

"What?" Elissa asked as she put the SUV in Drive.

"Nothing." But as she stared out the window at the coming twilight, Skyler almost laughed again at the idea of Logan asking anyone to marry him, especially someone as opposite to him as her.

Opposites attracted, didn't they?

She closed her eyes and leaned back against the headrest. But that didn't keep images of Logan from playing through her mind. She didn't have to admit it to her matchmaking friends, but he was pretty dang hot. Tall, with strong, wide shoulders, a naughty smile and dark hair that was made for a woman's hands to run through.

"You okay?" India asked.

Skyler's eyes popped open, and she hoped she hadn't made some sort of embarrassing sound. "Yeah, just tired. You know, the stress of jumping out of a plane and all. And so you know, I'm going to think up something really creative to get you all back."

"A lot of people say skydiving is the best thing they've ever done." India sounded so serious that Skyler figured Elissa and probably Verona were the driving force behind the matchmaking. No surprise there.

"Oh, I'm not talking about that. I'm talking about the whole convincing-Jesse-to-fake-being-sick thing."

India's eyes widened. "How did you figure that out?"

"Verona is not as sly as she thinks she is. And neither one of you seemed overly surprised when Jesse said he spent the morning hurling."

India smacked Elissa on the shoulder.

"Ow!"

"I told you I wasn't good at lying."

"Turns out we didn't have to be."

When they got back to Blue Falls, Elissa didn't head to the

inn. Instead, she pulled into an empty parking space next to the Blue Falls Music Hall.

"Come on, girls. No birthday is complete without a little dancing."

Part of Skyler wanted to protest, to go back to the inn and end the day with a glass of wine on her balcony. But despite her friends' shenanigans, she'd still had a good time with them today. She might as well end the day with a little dancing before she returned to the inn and got sucked back into work.

But when they stepped inside, Skyler considered asking Elissa to take her home. The place was wall-to-wall people, many of them obviously cowboys in town for the upcoming rodeo Liam had organized.

And right in the middle of them stood Logan Bradshaw and his cocky smile. That man was walking, talking trouble, and Skyler fought the urge to turn on her heel and leave. She did shift and eye her friends.

"What?" Elissa said. "It's a small town, and not like there are a lot of places to go at night."

"You know I don't believe for a minute you had nothing to do with him being here."

"Is there a problem with me being here?" The rumble of Logan's voice close behind her made Skyler's nerves hum.

He had the kind of voice that could coax the clothes off a woman. Heck, she halfway wanted to start tossing articles of clothing right there in the middle of the music hall. Like she'd thought, Trouble with a capital *T.*

She took a step away from him before she turned to face Logan. "No. It's a public place."

He wore a knowing grin that told her he didn't believe her nonchalance any more than she believed her friends hadn't invited him here.

But why was she fighting it so hard? It wasn't as though

this was going to be a fall-in-love-forever match. It was her birthday; why shouldn't she dance with a sexy man?

"You here to drink and socialize or do you actually know how to dance?" she asked.

He smiled and extended his hand. "Why don't you come with me and find out?"

Skyler hesitated a moment, feeling as if she was playing with a white-hot fire, before she placed her hand in Logan's and allowed him to lead her through the crowd to the middle of the wooden dance floor.

When he spun her into his arms, she'd swear her heart skipped a beat. It wasn't as if she'd never danced with a man, even good-looking ones, but there was something crazy intoxicating about Logan. It felt a little as if he'd fritzed her common sense and she didn't mind. Who knew there was a little hidden part of her that wanted to throw all her normal caution out the window and live free and wild for a night?

"So, do anything else adventurous today, birthday girl?" Logan guided her through the dancing couples without taking his eyes off her.

"No, jumping out of a plane pretty much used up my adventure quota for the year. That and dancing with perfect strangers."

His lips quirked up at the edge. "You think I'm perfect?"

She cocked her head to the side a little. "You're full of yourself, aren't you?"

"I live life to the fullest. Nothing wrong with that in my book."

"So you make jumping out of planes a habit, then?"

"When I can. That and deep-sea diving, backpacking, rappelling, riding bulls."

She looked up from where her gaze had been resting on the third button down his shirt. "You're here for the rodeo?"

"Didn't the hat and boots give it away?"

"It's Texas. Those don't exactly qualify as unusual."

"True."

So he was in Blue Falls for the rodeo. At least now she knew when he was probably leaving town. If she ended up flirting a little, no harm done. She wouldn't have to worry about backpedaling later. He'd be off to some other rodeo risking his neck.

She glanced to her left in time to see Liam and India dance by in the opposite direction. Neither of them paid her any attention, wrapped up as they were in each other. The music hall could empty out around them and the music stop, and they wouldn't notice. A pang of envy squeezed her middle. Despite the emotional ups and downs of her parents' marriage, she couldn't deny that there was a hidden romantic streak in her that wanted the kind of love Liam and India had, the kind that was pure, honest, that you didn't have to worry about. The kind that wouldn't up and disappear one day.

"You okay?"

Skyler jerked her attention back to Logan. "Yeah." She forced herself not to explain, or she might start babbling.

"So your friend and Liam are together?"

"India, yeah. They're getting married soon."

"Another one bites the dust."

Skyler stiffened involuntarily. She shouldn't be surprised he had such a dim view of marriage. Hadn't she thought as much about him earlier? She forced herself to relax, at least as much as she could in her current situation.

"You know Liam from the rodeo circuit?"

"Yeah, we've crossed paths a few times. Was surprised to see he'd moved to the little town where my cousin lives."

"Probably no more surprised than Liam and India were."

The song ended, but Logan didn't let her go, instead pulling her along with him as the next song began. "That's enough about other people. Let's talk about you, Skyler Harrington."

"What about me?"

"Like what you think about me."

Skyler laughed, unable to help herself.

"Look at that, she can smile."

"I smile."

"You had me wondering earlier today."

"I don't typically smile when I'm scared half out of my mind."

He leaned closer, robbing her of breath. "Come on, admit it. You liked it."

She was tempted to deny it, but then again, why? "Okay, fine. It was beautiful."

"So are you."

"I'm guessing these smooth lines usually work for you, don't they?"

"That's not a line. It's the truth."

When she looked up into his dark eyes, she believed him. Flustered, she lowered her gaze back down to the blue checkered shirt he wore. "Thank you."

Her nerves sizzled as Logan's arm slid around her and eased her closer. As the last strands of another song faded, Logan leaned close to her ear.

"I think I owe you an ice-cream cone." It was the most innocent of sentences, but the rich timbre of his voice that close to her ear made her go all gooey inside. He had her thinking things that were totally out of character for her.

"They have ice cream at the bar."

"I was thinking we ditch the crowd and walk down to the Ice Cream Hut."

Why did everything that came out of this man's mouth make her think of writhing in sheets, sweaty skin and tangled limbs? For heaven's sake, he was talking about ice cream.

For just the two of them.

Under the stars.

When she looked up at him, her eyes focused on his lips. His full, oh-so-kissable lips. "I don't think that's a good idea." She sounded breathless, probably because she was.

"Why not?" He said it close enough that she could feel his warm breath brush against her cheek.

She swallowed hard, searching for words that refused to form in her brain. She opened her mouth, but nothing came out.

Logan smiled. "Do I make you nervous, birthday girl?"

"Yes." Great, the power of speech came back in time for her to embarrass herself.

"You know what I think?"

She shook her head, unable to look away from him.

"I think it's been very rude of me not to give you a birthday present."

"You don't even know me."

Something flickered in his eyes, something that made her hyperaware of everywhere his body touched hers.

"I know enough."

And then those lips of his came closer and closer until they captured hers.

She knew she should resist, but she couldn't. When he deepened the kiss, Skyler decided that this was the best birthday ever.

Chapter Three

He'd died and gone to sensory-overload heaven. Logan pulled Skyler close, splaying his hand along the small of her back. What he'd meant to be a playful kiss went deeper because he suddenly couldn't get enough of the taste of her. Her curves fit nicely against him, and his blood pumped faster at the thought of seeing all those curves the way they were meant to be seen.

She broke the kiss but didn't back away. He took that as a good sign, that and the drugged look in her eyes.

"Hey, everybody!"

Skyler jerked back a step as her attention spun toward the stage. Her friend Elissa stood at the microphone.

"We've got a big birthday in the house tonight."

"I'm going to kill her," Skyler said under her breath.

He leaned close to her. "You said that already."

She glanced up at him. "Well, this time I mean it."

"We've got a special surprise for Skyler Harrington if she's not too busy," Elissa said, eliciting a few laughs from the crowd.

He chuckled, too, at the teasing look on Elissa's face.

Skyler thumped the back of her hand against his upper arm. "Cut it out. You're already on my list."

"Depending on the list, I might want to be on it."

Skyler's fair skin betrayed her as a blush crept up from her neck to her cheeks.

"You're even prettier when you blush."

"Hush." The way she said it with her gaze averted made him believe that she actually liked the compliment but didn't want to admit it.

He'd never claim to be an expert on women, but he couldn't help thinking that Skyler just might be worth the effort to learn more. She may try to hide it, but he got the feeling there was an entirely different Skyler Harrington simmering below the surface.

Movement at the edge of the stage turned out to be another woman carrying a birthday cake complete with lit candles.

"Okay, everybody together now," Elissa said, then launched into a rousing rendition of "Happy Birthday."

Even as Skyler's cheeks flamed redder, Logan joined in. Thank goodness it was a short song or Skyler might actually combust. As the song ended, everyone clapped and Skyler was urged to the stage. She walked as if she were heading to the gallows. He couldn't decide if he wanted to laugh or wrap her in his arms and hurry her away from the crowd that was making her so uncomfortable.

Well, wasn't that a gallant thought, so unlike him. He wasn't a jerk when it came to women, but he'd never been a knight in shining armor either.

Gradually, the crowd filled in the space between him and Skyler as she accepted a piece of cake and was surrounded by her friends. After a couple of minutes, the music started up again and he made his way to the bar. He'd barely gotten his beer and turned around to see if he could spot Skyler in the throng when Verona stepped up next to him.

"You and Skyler seemed to be having a nice time," she said.

"We were."

"That's good. She needs a night where she can loosen up a little."

Logan didn't respond beyond a grunt that indicated he'd heard her.

"You think you'll be staying long?"

"Just till the rodeo's done."

"Oh, that's too bad. Blue Falls is a nice place to settle down. You could ask Liam about that. He seems to like it."

"I'm not much of the staying-in-one-place type, ma'am. Can't make much money riding bulls if you don't go where the bulls are."

"I guess not." Verona sounded as if he'd shot the air out of her very pretty balloon.

He glanced in her direction to find her scanning the crowd. He got the oddest feeling she'd stricken his name from a list and was already seeking out a new potential mate for Skyler. And damned if that didn't make him angry.

Not for himself. What he'd told her was the truth. He was just annoyed on Skyler's behalf. If she was the least bit like him, she didn't like other people trying to carve out her life for her. Before he slipped and told a woman old enough to be his mother to mind her own business, he took another swig of his half-finished beer and set it on the counter behind him.

"If you'll excuse me." Before Verona could respond, he pushed his way into the crowd, intent on finding Skyler. The night was young, with plenty of time for more dancing and hopefully a few more kisses.

But by the time he made it to the middle of the dance floor, he noticed she was no longer near the stage. He searched the faces around him and finally spotted her heading out the front door as if the place was on fire.

Something told him he should let her go, that if he followed her, he would be getting in over his head. That thought was still repeating in his mind as his feet carried him toward the exit.

WHEN SKYLER STEPPED outside the music hall, she inhaled deeply and let it out slowly, what felt like the first true breath she'd taken since arriving. Between the crush of people, kissing Logan and then having every eye in the place turned toward her, she'd felt more and more of her breath stolen with each passing moment.

She still couldn't believe she'd kissed Logan, someone she'd met only hours ago, right there in the middle of the dance floor. And it wasn't just a peck either. It'd been a mind-melting, blow-her-shoes-off type of kiss. Whatever else she might say about Logan Bradshaw, the man could kiss. When his arms had pulled her close against his hard body, she'd wanted much more than kissing. Honestly, her body still hummed with that insane longing. For a crazy moment, she'd wished she was the type of carefree person who could indulge her yearnings without thinking it to death.

"Making a getaway before they spring another surprise on you?"

The sound of Logan's voice sent a little extra jolt to that hum within her, kicking it up a notch.

She glanced toward where he stood leaning back against someone's pickup truck. "That obvious, huh?"

He held up one hand with his thumb and forefinger nearly together. "A touch."

"Did they send you out here to drag me back in?"

"Nope. I'm chasing you because I still intend to buy you that ice-cream cone."

"I just had cake. The last thing I need is ice cream."

"Don't tell me you're worried about your figure. Because from where I'm standing, you're an entire ice-cream factory away from having to worry about it."

Though it wouldn't be visible out here in the half light of the parking lot, Skyler's face heated at his compliment. Despite the fact that compliments probably rolled off his tongue easily because he had a lot of practice, there was a ring of truth behind his words. It might be a line, but it wasn't a lie, at least not from his point of view. That made her stupidly happy.

Logan pushed away from the truck and walked slowly toward her. "Come on, you know you can't resist the siren call of ice cream."

Skyler laughed. "You're used to getting whatever you want, aren't you?"

Logan smiled, and it made her heart do a funny little flip.

"Good things come to those who go after them." He leaned toward her and lowered his voice to a whisper. "And just so you know, right now that good thing isn't the ice cream."

"What is?"

His eyes took on a wicked gleam, the kind of wicked that tempted you to do things you'd never normally consider, not outside of your imagination, anyway. "I think you know."

Her breath caught trying to escape her lungs. He was going to kiss her again, and oh how she wanted him to do exactly that. Only he didn't. Instead, he slid his fingers through hers and started leading her down the sidewalk.

She searched frantically for something to say but came up empty. Was she being totally nuts, walking off into the night with a stranger without telling anyone where she was going? But it was as if a part of her that never revealed itself was in charge, telling her to enjoy the moment, the feel of his strong hand wrapped around hers, the high of having a good-looking man showing interest in her.

Sure, she went out from time to time, less than Elissa but more than India ever had, but this felt different. Electric and breathless and exciting. She had a good life, one she enjoyed, but this type of excitement never made an appearance in her safe, ordered life. She'd never known she yearned for it. Part of her still believed none of this could be real, that she had to be dreaming.

When they reached the Ice Cream Hut, Logan led her to the window. "Get whatever you want."

Mari Brewer, the teenage daughter of Larena Brewer, the inn's head chef, saw Skyler first. Then her eyes widened when she spotted Logan. It seemed to take a good bit of effort for her to shift her gaze back to Skyler.

"Hey, happy birthday. Sorry I couldn't make it to the party."

"Thanks, and don't worry about it. I just made a quick getaway."

"Don't blame you." The way Mari looked at Logan, it was obvious she would have chosen time alone with the hot guy over a building full of people, too.

"Blue Falls is growing on me." Logan placed one hand along the lower part of Skyler's back but propped the other forearm along the ledge outside the serving window. "Seems every woman I meet here is pretty."

Mari smiled and laughed a little.

"Cut it out," Skyler said, and nudged him in the ribs with her elbow. "We're here for ice cream, not for you to hone your flirting skills."

Instead of behaving, Logan leaned closer to the window and Mari. "Sorry, beautiful, but I think she wants me all for herself."

Skyler rolled her eyes. "You are impossible. Mari, can I get a scoop of blueberry, please?"

"Sure." Mari looked at Logan. "And for you?"

"Vanilla."

When Mari turned to scoop the ice cream, Skyler faced Logan. "Vanilla, really? You don't seem like a plain vanilla sort of guy."

He shrugged. "Maybe I'm sweet enough without all the fancy flavors."

Skyler snorted. "*Sweet* is not the word that comes to mind."

"Then what word does?"

Skyler accepted her ice-cream cone. "You can just keep wondering about that one."

A stream of words scrolled through her mind, but three stood out brighter and bolder and truer than all the rest. *Sexy... as...sin.*

But he knew that, so she wasn't about to pad his ego by admitting her thoughts out loud. Instead, she left him waiting for his ice cream and headed toward one of the benches that sat next to the lake. The moon was rising, its reflection glittering on the surface of the water.

When Logan joined her, he sat close enough to put his arm around her. Part of her told her to shift away, but that was the part that was always so careful. Though she couldn't explain it, tonight she wanted to pretend she was someone else, someone who wasn't so wrapped up in the "right" way to do everything.

"This is nice," he said after several moments went by.

She took a deep breath of the cooler night air. "Yes, it is."

"More your speed than jumping out of airplanes?"

She smiled and glanced at him. "Understatement of the century."

"Bet you never expected to enjoy it."

She refocused on the water and really thought about it. Skydiving wasn't something she would have done on her own, too many things that could go wrong, but was she glad she'd been forced into it?

"No. I still get nauseated when I think about actually doing it, but the view was incredible."

He bumped his shoulder into hers. "See, not so bad living a little."

"I live just fine, thank you." She took another bite of her ice cream, hurrying to keep it from melting down the sides of the cone and all over her hand.

"That right? So what do you do on days when you're not jumping out of planes?"

She wiped her mouth with a napkin. "I own the Wildflower Inn." She pointed across the lake at the lights of the inn.

"That right? How many beds there?"

Skyler looked up at Logan just as he licked his ice cream. Good grief, that action made her sizzle all over. "Um…" What was she trying to remember? Oh, yeah, number of beds at the inn. She imagined Logan lying on one of those soft fluffy beds.

The lights on the Ice Cream Hut went out, cloaking Skyler and Logan in darkness. It was enough to jerk her out of her careening thoughts, ones so unlike her it was as if she'd suddenly discovered another personality inside herself.

"Thirty," she finally remembered to say. "Well, thirty rooms. Some are singles, some doubles, a mixture."

Logan chuckled. "I do make you nervous."

"Yes." *Way to go, admit it again, give him even more ammunition. Make yourself look like more of a ninny.*

Unable to sit still, she jumped to her feet and walked toward the garbage can to toss her trash.

"What, you don't like cones?" Logan asked.

"No. I like to eat ice cream out of them but don't like the cones themselves. I know, weird quirk."

"We all have them."

"Oh, yeah? What's your quirk?"

He took the crunchy last bite of his cone, chewed slowly, making her nervous as he watched her without answering, then swallowed. "I like redheads."

She laughed. "And blondes, and brunettes."

He got to his feet and walked toward her. When he stood less than an arm's length away, he reached around her to pitch his napkin. "But redheads who like blueberry ice cream most of all."

Skyler laughed and realized that despite his corny lines and cocky self-assurance, she liked him. He was good for a laugh.

And for kissing.

As if he could read her thoughts, Logan pulled her to him and lowered his lips to hers. Beyond the blueberry flavor coating her tongue, she tasted the vanilla. Something about the mixing of flavors sent a burst of heat through her and had her hands finding their way up his chest. Even through the fabric, she could tell he had the kind of chest that made covering it with a shirt a crime.

She moaned into his mouth at the thought, and that seemed to toss fuel on the fire beginning to blaze between them. Logan pulled her even closer, so close that she felt his arousal. If she'd thought she was buzzing with desire before, that had been nothing compared to the zing that went through her now.

His hands ran up her ribs and brushed the underside of her breasts. She gasped, but another kiss captured her surprise.

The sound of a car starting barely registered, but when light suddenly illuminated them, Skyler startled enough to end the kiss and take a step back from Logan. Right as loud music filled the night air, Skyler realized the car belonged to Mari and she'd gotten a good show as she left work for the evening.

Skyler spun away, turning her back toward Mari's car. Not that it mattered. Her face was likely flaming enough to light up the night more than Mari's headlights.

As Mari took off, letting the darkness settle again, Logan walked up behind Skyler. Trying to gather up some common sense, she didn't give him the opportunity to pull her to him again.

"I need to get back before India and Elissa call out the cavalry."

He didn't argue but rather took a step back and extended his hand toward the sidewalk, inviting her to proceed ahead of him. She took a shaky step then another. Her nerves continued to buzz even though Logan didn't make any attempt to touch her. How crazy was it that she already missed the feel of his hand around hers, the warmth of his body pressed against hers?

Still, crazy or not, she couldn't get the idea out of her head as they walked past businesses closed for the night. The closer they came to the music hall, the more she slowed her pace, knowing that when they reached the hall, that would be the end of being with Logan. And despite the fact they were little more than strangers and he was too cocky for his own good, she couldn't deny he made her feel like no man ever had, daring and wonderfully nervous and…alive.

She might have lost her mind, but she didn't want to lose that other Skyler quite yet. It was her birthday, after all, and it was time she gave herself a present. As they reached the narrow opening between Tumbleweed Books and Rand's Western Wear where the city had built a tiny park, Skyler stopped walking.

"Something wrong?" Logan asked.

For a long moment, she said nothing, just stared at the sidewalk while an argument took place in her head. Her normal, sensible self said her day had been filled with enough excitement already and it was time to return to real life. But an increasingly loud voice told her that it felt good to really live, that it was still her birthday and she should enjoy it to the fullest.

"Skyler?" Logan sounded concerned this time, and that sealed the deal.

She grabbed the front of his shirt with both of her hands and dragged him into the darker confines of the little park. She pushed him up against the side of the bookstore and captured his lips with hers, filling her senses with him.

Logan wasted no time returning the kiss, spinning so that

her back was against the wall. He pressed his body close, every bit as eager as she was. His hands slid under her shirt and skimmed along the sensitive skin of her sides and then up her spine.

Skyler somehow gathered enough brain cells together to realize they had to go somewhere or they were going to end up naked against the side of a building. That thought half scared her, half excited her even more than she already was.

"Do you want to come back to the inn with me?" She breathed the words against his mouth. They sounded as though they were coming from someone else, certainly not careful-to-a-fault Skyler Harrington. But she couldn't deny she wanted this man and she wanted him now.

Logan's mouth moved from her lips, up her jaw to her ear. He captured her earlobe with his teeth, not hard enough to hurt, just enough to make her arch against him. "My motel room's closer."

Something low in her belly, lower even than that, screamed yes. But Skyler hesitated, a sliver of the person she really was trying to assert itself.

Logan moved away enough that she could look up into his eyes. He lifted a hand and smoothed her hair behind her ear in a surprisingly tender gesture. He probably didn't think anything of it, but that simple movement tipped the scales away from caution toward total abandon.

Skyler entwined her fingers through his and followed the part of herself she'd never known existed, the part that had gone through with jumping out of that plane, the part that would likely disappear with the morning light. But that was still hours away.

"Lead the way."

Chapter Four

The music and laughter coming from the music hall faded as Skyler allowed Logan to lead her off of Main Street onto Seven Hills Avenue. Her heartbeat thundered louder and harder with every step they took away from the music hall, her friends, safety in numbers. Her step faltered as they came within view of the Country Vista Inn, a little strip of a motel frequented more by cowboys and road-maintenance crews than tourists. It wasn't a dump, just not the Wildflower Inn. The Country Vista served its purpose, giving people a place to sleep.

Or something else.

Logan stopped and spun her into his arms. "Don't think too much."

"I don't know. I—"

He halted her words by capturing her mouth with his and overwhelming her senses with pure, undiluted desire. She felt that kiss zing along all of her veins like a hit of some intoxicating drug she was powerless to resist. As Logan started walking backward without breaking the kiss, her feet followed. When he finally broke the kiss, her body buzzed with need as her thoughts swirled like a hurricane in her head.

When they reached the door to his room, her common sense made one final desperate attempt to stop her. But the moment Logan slid his key card through the reader and opened the door to his room, allowing her to see the king-size bed, she was lost.

Logan led her inside and locked the door behind her. In the next moment, he backed her against the door and kissed her again. This time his hands slid down her ribs to rest on her hips. When he pressed closer, Skyler gasped at his obvious arousal. Logan chuckled against her lips as his hands untucked her T-shirt. When the callused texture of his palm made contact with her skin, she recaptured his mouth.

She'd never wanted to have sex so much in her life. Logan could consume her right now, and she wouldn't care. In fact, she'd welcome it.

The next thing she knew, Logan grasped the bottom of her shirt and quickly pulled it over her head. Before she could catch her breath, he lowered his wet, warm mouth to the swell of her breast above her bra. She grabbed the hat still on his head and tossed it onto a chair in the corner, then ran her hands through his hair, pulling him closer.

Logan unsnapped her bra, allowing him to nudge the fabric aside and capture her breast in his mouth.

"Oh, yes."

She felt him smile against her, probably because it was obvious she'd never done anything like this before. But then he flicked the sensitive tip with his tongue, and her eyes closed as she pressed her head back against the door. As Logan shifted his talented mouth from one breast to the other, Skyler's legs shook.

"You need to get off your feet," Logan whispered in her ear. Then he scooped her up into his arms and carried her to the bed. He lay her crossways on the mattress, then followed her down.

She realized she'd lost her bra when Logan captured one of her breasts again, then wrapped his arms around her to lift her closer to his mouth. Her hands gripped the back of his shirt, pulling it up so that she could run her hands over his naked flesh.

Her body warmed even more as she ran her fingers across all that taut skin over well-defined muscles.

Logan lifted himself and smiled down at her. "Let me help you with that." Without breaking eye contact, he unbuttoned his shirt and tossed it aside as if he didn't care whether he ever saw it again.

Forget a crime. It would be a sin to cover up that chest. Every woman was turned on by different parts of a man, and for her it was definitely chests and arms. And Logan's were perfect—tanned, toned, with the kind of muscle definition that came from hard work rather than pumping iron.

Logan's mouth quirked up at one end. "Like the view?"

Skyler licked her lips. "Yes."

Logan smiled wider as he lowered himself to her mouth, kissing her deeply as his hands went to the top of her jeans and slipped the button free. Her breath came faster as he lowered her zipper and slid his hand inside the top edge of her panties.

A five-alarm fire started in her middle and flashed out to the tips of her extremities in the blink of an eye. Unwilling to wait any longer for what her body craved, Skyler found the top of Logan's jeans and mimicked what he'd done to hers. When she slid her hands inside to cup his naked hips, Logan growled against her lips.

He rolled away only long enough to pull off his boots and rid himself of the rest of his clothing. Then he made quick work of making her every bit as naked as he was.

Mercy, he was gorgeous, from head to toe. And gone was their relatively slow progress. She shocked herself by watching his every movement as he ripped open a foil package and sheathed himself. If possible, she grew even hotter and needier at the sight. She found it difficult to breathe, as if her lungs were as stunned by the view before her as she was.

Logan lowered himself to the bed and pulled her beneath him, nudging her legs apart with his knee. He kissed her again, his tongue dancing with hers and making her wonder how she'd ever made it through a day without being kissed like that.

"Are you okay?" he asked as he trailed kisses across her cheek toward her ear.

"I'm not sure. I feel like I'm going to burst into flames."

Logan gripped her hips and pulled her up to press against his erection. "The feeling's mutual." He teased at her opening for just a moment before he plunged inside her, filling her as she'd never, ever been filled before.

A new wave of desire surged through her, prompting her to move against him, yearning for more. His hands splayed against her hips, he pulled her body to meet his as he drove into her again. Without thinking, Skyler wrapped her legs around him and captured Logan's mouth, kissing, tugging, biting until she had to throw her head back in order to get enough air into her lungs. She gasped as Logan increased his pace, and she began meeting each of his thrusts with ones of her own.

Vibrations started deep within her, and she dug her hands into Logan's hair. She didn't need to say a word for him to know she wanted to increase the pace. With each stroke, she felt herself getting closer to the pinnacle. Her breath came faster as she bowed up against Logan's straining body.

"Yes, yes, yes," she said before she reached her peak.

Logan, who must have been hanging on to his own release with tight reins until she found hers, made one final stroke, then went rigid all over. He cried out as he found completion, then collapsed half on, half off her. He sucked in great gulps of air.

They didn't speak. As the raging desire and physical bliss faded and Skyler was left with listening to the breathing of a near stranger next to her, she wondered if she truly had gone insane.

LOGAN FELT THE moment Skyler began to think too much, when she started slipping back to the woman she'd been before she'd made the decision to take a chance and live a little. Well, he couldn't have that, because if he had his way, the night was far from over for them.

He wrapped his hand around the curve of her hip and rolled her to face him. "Stop."

"Stop what?"

"Thinking."

"I can't." Her voice held a hint of panic at the edge.

"Well, I have a cure for that." He pulled her closer, draping her leg over his hip as he captured her sweet mouth with his. She still tasted like her blueberry ice cream.

He sensed a moment of resistance in her before she caved and ran her soft fingertips up his chest. Her hand stopped moving when she reached the puckered skin on his left pec. She leaned away and ran her finger along the slash.

"What happened to you?"

"A bull I was riding didn't particularly like me."

Her mouth fell open on a little gasp. "A horn did this?"

"Hazard of the job."

She looked up at him, and his breath caught. Even in the dim light and with her hair tousled, she was stunning. He hadn't lied—he did love redheads. He'd dare any man to see Skyler Harrington and not want to take her straight to his bed.

"You've got a death wish, don't you?"

He smiled. "Not at all. I very much like living, especially right now." Before she could speak or think any more, he ran his hand along her jaw and into her hair and brought her tasty mouth to his again. No matter how much he kissed her, he couldn't seem to get enough. He never lacked for female companionship, but it had been a long time since he'd craved a woman as he did Skyler.

The mere touch of her hands skimming along the skin of his chest drove him wild, and he rolled her onto her back. As he slid home again, one word echoed in his head. *Perfect*.

SKYLER PULLED THE cover over her shoulder as she gradually came awake. Why did the air-conditioning feel so cold? And why was it running so loudly? She opened her eyes and blinked a couple of times. It took a few seconds for the confusion to fade enough for her to realize what she was looking at—a motel air-conditioning unit.

She froze as another cog slipped into place, the one telling her that the reason she had awakened chilled was the fact that she was still naked. She closed her eyes and tried to calm her breathing. Bad move. Closing her eyes only gave her a blank screen on which to replay what had happened with Logan. She'd had mind-blowing sex, twice, with a man she'd met that morning.

She glanced at the clock. Correction, yesterday morning. It wasn't her birthday anymore, so that meant it was time to get her temporarily insane self out of this room and away from Logan Bradshaw and his delectable body.

Somehow she was able to calm her panic enough to listen to his breathing. Slow, steady, definitely asleep. She held her breath as she eased out from under the covers and carefully retrieved and put on her clothes. When Logan stirred in his sleep, she stopped dead. She made the mistake of looking at him. His bare chest tempted her to crawl back into bed and wake him in a way he would be sure to appreciate. The way the sheet rode low around his hips caused her to lick her lips at the memory of him making love to her.

No, it was sex. Making love was something you did with someone you actually cared about, not a stranger who'd probably done this same thing with countless other women. Thank goodness they'd at least been safe about it.

Even though she knew she should go, her feet weren't getting the message. Instead, she stood and watched him sleep. The part of her that had led her here, the part that likely wouldn't exist outside this room, whispered that she'd done nothing wrong. That she deserved to enjoy herself, to revel in the feel of a man's body pressed close to hers. And Logan's had felt like nothing she'd ever imagined. If she let herself, she could get used to that feeling.

But it wasn't real. This wasn't her, and he would be gone in a matter of days.

That's what India thought about Liam.

She shook her head to clear away the thought. Logan was nothing like Liam. India's fiancé was a hardworking father and business owner. Logan had that carefree adrenaline-junkie vibe. Chances were he wouldn't live to be an old man. That scar across his chest was evidence of that. Nothing but pure sexual hunger had brought her to this room, because other than the physical desire, they were absolutely nothing alike.

Her common sense slammed back into her as if it had taken a short vacation, and suddenly she needed to get far away from Logan Bradshaw as quickly as possible. She pushed aside one final surge of yearning and slipped out the door into the night. Before anyone who might recognize her noticed her, she hurried across the lit parking lot to the dimmer sidewalk that led back toward Main Street.

With each hurried step away from the motel, she scolded herself more for her incredible lapse in judgment. She'd just had sex with a near stranger, twice! She wanted to get home, take a shower and go to bed. If she was supremely lucky, in the morning she'd wake up and this would all be nothing more than a hot, steamy dream.

As she neared downtown, she slowed as her thoughts spun. How in the world was she going to face Elissa and India? Why hadn't she gone back to the music hall as she'd intended? Dealing with their matchmaking attempts would have been more bearable than telling them she'd gone off to the Country Vista to have sex with her skydiving partner. Wondering why she hadn't heard from them, she stopped walking and pulled out her phone. When she saw she had twelve unanswered text messages, she remembered she'd put her phone on silent during the movie and had forgotten to change it back. If only she'd had the ringer on, maybe the texts would have kept her from making the biggest mistake of her life.

She scrolled through them.

Elissa: Hope you're having a good time with Mr. McHottiePants.

Elissa: Smooch, smooch, smooch.

India: Ignore her. Call if you need us.

Several more followed in the same vein before India's final message:

Where are you? Are you ok? Let me know.

She glanced across the street toward the mostly empty parking lot of the Blue Falls Music Hall and knew she couldn't face seeing either of her friends tonight. With a deep breath, she texted India back.

Fine. Sorry, forgot to turn the ringer back on. Tired, heading to bed.

Just as soon as she walked the mile and a half around the lake to her apartment. If she made it without someone seeing her and setting the local gossip mill ablaze, she'd officially be the luckiest woman in all of the Hill Country.

She hurried toward the walking path that circled the lake. When she passed the Ice Cream Hut, she couldn't help but remember how Logan had teased both her and Mari as if it were the easiest thing in the world. Damn her hormones—it probably was. She imagined him buying an ice-cream cone for a woman in every rodeo town he rolled into. Tears pooled in her eyes, and that made her even angrier. But she wasn't angry at Logan. He hadn't claimed to be anything he wasn't. No, she was angry at herself. She'd let her body trump the orderly, precise thought process that had gotten her through years of upheaval and allowed her to become a successful businesswoman.

She increased her pace, wanting to be home more than she could express. Her anger grew, extending to her friends. They'd pushed her to the point where she'd fallen prey to Logan's good looks and smooth talking. All the way back to the inn, she concocted countless ways to get back at them. But that would mean admitting what had happened. And by the time she unlocked the exterior door to her apartment that wouldn't necessitate her walking through the inn's lobby, she'd decided she was keeping her one-night stand to herself. That shouldn't be a problem, since she couldn't imagine Logan caring enough to deliberately cross her path again. He'd had her, and most likely he'd be on to the next woman who caught his eye.

That last thought kept reverberating in her head as she made straight for her bathroom and took a shower. Why did it bother her so much?

Because she wasn't one to give even her body so easily.

She'd lost control, and if there was one thing she couldn't bear, it was to not be in control of her own life.

She dressed in cool summer pajamas and crawled into her bed. She inhaled the familiar clean scent of it, ran her hand across the downy softness. Everything about it was better than the bed at the Country Vista Inn.

Except that she was alone. She tried to tell herself that she was perfectly fine on her own, that she preferred it that way. But as a tear finally leaked out and trailed down to her pillow, she admitted that she was lonely. Logan wasn't to blame for what happened between them. Her friends weren't either. It was the loneliness that most of the time she could convince herself was a figment of her imagination, the empty feeling that she rarely acknowledged. But as she lay in her bed alone, she let herself feel it. She let herself admit, if only to herself in the privacy of her own mind, that she missed the warmth of a man's body next to her.

As she closed her eyes, she allowed herself to relive every moment, every touch she'd shared with Logan. Moments and touches that had for a short while made her forget that loneliness.

Chapter Five

Logan knew Skyler was gone even before he opened his eyes. The room was too quiet and the bed next to him too cool for her to still be there. He looked at the rumpled sheet where she'd lain. It wasn't a surprise she was gone, but he had to admit it was a disappointment. Finding his way into her body again this morning would have been a great way to start the day. But he guessed he was lucky she'd stayed as long as she had, that she'd agreed to come back to the room with him at all.

If he were to place a bet, he'd say she was drowning in regret this morning. He wondered if he shouldn't have pressed her so much, but then he remembered how she'd pulled him into that dark little park and kissed him as if her soul depended on it. She might not admit it, but she'd wanted what they'd shared just as much as he had.

Suddenly ravenous, he rolled out of bed, took a shower, dressed and headed for the Primrose Café. He'd worked up quite an appetite with Skyler. Maybe he'd even see her in town this morning and cause her to blush with a kiss in broad daylight. He smiled at that thought. If Skyler was regretting going to bed with him, maybe he should make it his mission to erase that regret. And get her right back in that bed. Whatever she might say the day after, they'd been good together.

Who knew there was that much fire under the surface of Miss Prim and Proper?

When he stepped through the front door of the café, a quick survey of the room showed every table was full. A young waitress with a dirty plate in one hand and a coffeepot in the other stopped next to him on her way across the dining room.

"There's still a couple of stools left up front," she said with a nod toward the counter lined with stools.

She was probably in her mid-twenties with a long brown ponytail. He recognized the smile on her pink lips and the look of appreciation in her bright blue eyes. Normally he would have returned them as his thoughts shifted away from breakfast. But for some reason, in his mind the waitress's face was replaced by Skyler's.

Feeling a bit off, he nodded. "I'll take a cup of that coffee when you get the chance."

"Be right there as soon as I take care of the Chew the Fat Club."

He watched as she headed toward the front corner of the restaurant next to the big picture window that had Primrose Café painted across it. Four old coots were deep in conversation, likely solving all the world's problems. Logan laughed a little under his breath. There seemed to be a Chew the Fat Club in every small town in America. Those guys probably had a dozen grandkids between them and were here every morning drinking their weight in coffee. And by the way they smiled when the waitress approached, probably part of what they talked about during their morning get-togethers was the good old days when they'd been wild bucks chasing pretty girls.

Pretty girls like Skyler Harrington.

Logan shook his head and crossed to the stool at the end of the bar. He needed an entire pot of coffee to wake up and send his body and mind the message that it was a new day.

His hot night with Skyler was done. He didn't regret it, not one bit, but he wasn't one to get too wrapped up in any one woman. He didn't live the kind of life where that made a lick of sense. He slid onto the stool and grabbed a menu.

"Saw you at the music hall last night," the pretty waitress said as she set an empty cup in front of him. He glanced at her nametag. Gretchen.

"Yep. Seemed like the place to be."

"You know Skyler?"

There was more to her question than simple curiosity, and for some reason a voice in Logan's head told him to tread carefully. What was up with that?

"Met her and her friends yesterday." He pointed toward a photo on the menu. "I'll have the Good Morning Platter with scrambled eggs." Two eggs, bacon, sausage and a biscuit with gravy. His night with Skyler had left him with an enormous appetite this morning. That thought made him want to grin.

Gretchen jotted down his order and headed for the window to the kitchen. While her back was turned, someone slid onto the only remaining empty stool, next to him.

"Tell me I'm not going to have to sic the sheriff on you."

He glanced over to see Skyler's friend Elissa sitting next to him with a "Don't mess with me, or I'll eat you for lunch" expression on her face.

"Pardon?"

"The last time I saw or heard from Skyler, she was heading out the door of the music hall with you. Then, poof, she disappears. Doesn't answer calls, doesn't respond to texts, doesn't contact me for a ride home."

A twinge of worry hit him. "Have you tried her this morning?"

"Yes, but still no answer."

Had something happened to her? Blue Falls was one of those small towns where you didn't think anything bad ever happened, but the reality was that evil knew no geographic boundaries. "She was fine when I saw her last." She'd felt fine, too, snuggled up next to him for warmth, her soft curves making him want to take her all over again.

"What time was that?"

"I don't know, sometime after midnight."

The smile that started to spread across Elissa's face surprised him. It took a moment to realize he'd been maneuvered into revealing a little too much, probably way more than Skyler wanted out there in the light of day.

"You're a sneaky one," he said, unsure if he admired her ability or was annoyed by it.

"I had to do something. Skyler obviously isn't going to say anything."

"You've talked to her?"

"No. She's dodging my calls, and now I know why."

"But she's okay?" Something in him needed to know she was safe.

Elissa gave him a look that was a bit too probing. "Yeah. I called the inn, and she's there working as usual."

"You did hijack one of her work days." Strangely relieved to know Skyler was safe, he took a drink of his coffee.

"It was her birthday. No one should work on their birthday."

Gretchen returned and slid his plate in front of him. "Can I get you anything else?"

"Just keep the coffee coming, gorgeous."

Gretchen beamed, and something inside Logan told him he shouldn't have encouraged her.

"So you going to ask Skyler out again?" Elissa said, obviously timing her question so Gretchen would hear it.

Gretchen's smile dimmed some, though she tried to hide it. Then she was off to tend to other customers.

Logan took another slow drink of his coffee before turning his gaze toward Elissa. "Maybe."

"Be warned. She's probably going to try to avoid you like she is me."

"I can be persuasive when I want to be." And contrary to his normal M.O., he did want to see Skyler again. Maybe if he could coax her into bed one more time, he could get her out of his system and move on. Because that's exactly what he'd be doing after the rodeo in a few days, moving on.

"Good to know." With a satisfied smile, Elissa slid off her stool and headed toward the front door.

Logan dug into his breakfast as he considered how he might win over Skyler to his way of thinking, that they could have a lot of fun together while he was in town. As he scooped the last of his eggs into his mouth and downed the rest of his coffee, a plan slid into place. He tossed a generous tip down for Gretchen and headed toward the front door, a grin of confidence tugging at his lips.

SKYLER STARED INTO her bathroom mirror, trying to decide if there was any way someone could just look at her and know what she'd done the night before. It'd been a miracle she'd made it back to the inn without someone seeing her. Now all she had to do was act normal so she didn't end up telling on herself.

She shook her head, still not quite able to believe the night with Logan was real. But her body told her as soon as she'd woken that her time in his bed had been much more than a vivid dream. If she were the type of person to believe in such things, she would swear she'd been possessed by some sex-crazed maniac.

Well, there was no way to go back in time and erase her mistake, so she just had to go forward. She'd dive into work, occupy her mind with something other than the memory of

Logan Bradshaw's muscles straining above her in the dim light. Skyler closed her eyes and took several slow, deep breaths before leaving the bathroom and her reflection behind.

Work didn't totally take her mind off Logan, but at least it kept her busy. Other than doing the usual tasks that filled her day, she pulled out her sketches for the revitalized Wren Cove Park. As luck would have it, the cause benefiting from the upcoming rodeo was the rebuilding of the park at the bottom of the hill below her inn. Blue Falls families had picnicked and launched canoes from the park for decades until a flood two years ago had destroyed the dock and the picnic shelters. And because of budget cuts, the city hadn't been able to rebuild it.

In fact, the city council had been considering selling the property until Skyler suggested one of the new benefit rodeos be used to raise funds for the rebuilding of the park. When the city officials still hadn't been sure, she'd offered to attach the running of the park to that of her inn. The next thing she knew, she'd been agreeing to buy the property for a rock-bottom price with the understanding that she could use the rodeo proceeds for the rebuilding.

The moment she'd signed on the dotted line, she'd nearly had a panic attack. But India had managed to calm her, pointing out that she now had control to redesign the park however she liked. With that thought in her head, new ideas had started forming almost faster than she could write them down. She just didn't know how many of them would be feasible until the rodeo was over.

The rodeo she would have to go to, where she could run into Logan.

Somewhere, she imagined Fate laughing her ass off.

Skyler pushed the thought away and added a sand volleyball court at the edge of the park sketch. When she flubbed one of the lines, she erased the entire addition and started over. If the rodeo could generate enough money, hopefully she could get the work done and families could start enjoying the park by early- to mid-fall.

At the sound of approaching footsteps, she looked up. Elissa strode into the office and plopped herself down in the chair opposite Skyler's desk. India positioned herself behind the other chair and placed her hands on its back. Skyler got a really bad feeling in the pit of her stomach. She glanced back at Elissa, who sat with an expectant look on her face.

"What?" Skyler asked.

"You had sex with him, didn't you?"

Skyler's heart thumped extra hard as she looked out the office door to see if anyone was nearby who might have heard. "Oh, my God. Do you think you could talk a little louder?"

"You did, didn't you?" Elissa wasn't one to be easily steered off track.

"What are you talking about?"

"You disappeared with him and then didn't respond to any of our texts or calls."

Skyler gestured toward India. "I texted India back that I came home and was going to bed."

"Alone?"

"Yes, alone."

"I told you," India said.

Elissa looked confused. "That's not the impression I got from Logan."

Skyler stiffened. "What did he say?" She knew the moment the accusatory words left her mouth that she'd made a tactical error.

Elissa clapped her hands together. "I knew it!"

India rounded her chair and sat on the edge of the seat. "Are you okay?"

Skyler let out a sigh. "I'm fine, unless you count temporary insanity."

"What's insane about being with a drop-dead gorgeous guy?" Elissa asked.

"I just met him," Skyler said low so no one outside the office would hear.

"I told you all that holding back was going to blow up one of these days."

"Hush," India told Elissa.

"Why? I think it's great."

"You think it's great that I slept with a complete stranger?"

Elissa leaned forward. "Hon, you are wound up way too tight most of the time. Are you going to sit there and tell me that it didn't feel good to let go a little?"

"I wouldn't call that a little."

Elissa quirked a brow. "That so?"

Skyler leaned back in her chair and covered her face with her hands. "This isn't me."

"Precisely my point," Elissa said. "I'm not saying you become a serial bed hopper, but it's not healthy to be alone all the time, to be so tense about every little thing you do."

Skyler dropped her hands to her lap. "Well, I think I can mark off about ten years' worth of letting myself go, so you can stop worrying about it."

"Ten years. That good, huh?"

Skyler stared at her friend. "What do you want, a play-by-play?"

Elissa gave her an evil grin. "Only if you want to."

"Keep on wishing."

"You're no fun at all."

"I just want to forget it happened, and you're not helping."

"So he wasn't that good?"

"I didn't say that."

Elissa squealed, and even India smiled at that revelation.

"But it was a one-time thing, a mistake."

"Why is it a mistake?" India asked. "You were safe, right?"

"Of course. I'm not a complete idiot. It's just…I have a million other things that I need to focus on."

"You have to go to bed at some point," Elissa said. "Why do it alone?"

"Have you had someone warming your bed lately we don't know about?"

Elissa jerked a little at the question, making Skyler wonder if she'd hit a sore spot.

"No."

"Then maybe you don't need to concern yourself so much with who's in mine."

Elissa didn't have a comeback. In fact, she stood and headed for the door. "I've got to get to work."

Skyler stared at her friend as she left the office without another word. "Okay, did she just pull a Jekyll and Hyde right in front of me?"

India sighed. "I know she's a bit much. She drove me batty when she was trying to push Liam and me together, but I do think she means well."

"I know. I'm just rattled this morning. I felt like I was someone else last night."

A couple of moments passed before India spoke. "Maybe that's not such a bad thing. I didn't realize I was cutting myself off from everyone, from the possibility of getting hurt, until I was shoved out of my comfort zone. And it's been so worth it."

"Yeah, but this is different. Logan Bradshaw is not Liam."

"Maybe not, and maybe he's not the love of your life. But I also think that what happened isn't worth beating yourself up over. Maybe you were just lonely."

Skyler met India's eyes and realized that the quieter of her two best friends was that way for a reason. She was busy observing and seeing what others didn't. Skyler averted her eyes, unable to stand seeing the truth reflected back at her. She searched for something to say but came up empty.

India stood. "I think maybe you're not the only one who is lonely and doesn't know exactly how to deal with that loneliness."

Was she talking about Elissa? How could Elissa be lonely? If she ever wanted a date, she had one. The girl was almost always in a good mood and surrounded by people. But then, Skyler was often surrounded by people, too. She realized in that moment that there wasn't just one type of loneliness.

She looked up at India to find her friend had left the office while Skyler was lost in her own thoughts.

For the next hour, Skyler tried to refocus her mind on work, but it proved a waste of time. She kept thinking about how maybe she should consider opening herself up to finding someone to spend her life with, but every time she tried to imagine it the old fear came back. She liked her independence. It was comfortable, familiar, safe. Yes, there were times when she was lonely, but maybe she just needed to fill those hours with more projects, perhaps a new hobby. Anything that wouldn't let her down in the end, the way her father had her mother. The way... No, she didn't want to think about the past anymore. That's why it was the past. Done, finished, over with. You couldn't change it, so why dwell on it?

Why was she letting one lapse in judgment tie her up in knots and make her doubt all the other decisions she'd made in her life?

Feeling as if the walls of her office were closing in on her, she stood with the aim of walking down to the park for some fresh air and perhaps some new inspiration for her vision of what the park could become.

She headed up the hallway toward the lobby. She was a few steps into the lobby before she recognized the person standing at the front desk. Her mouth dropped open as Logan turned with an army duffel on his shoulder.

He smiled and damn if her knees didn't weaken a little. "Good morning," he said as he crossed toward her.

"What are you doing here?" She kept her voice low and tried not to appear as freaked out as she felt.

"I'm staying here."

"No, you're not. You're staying at the Country Vista." She needed him to stay at the Country Vista, well away from her and her traitorous hormones.

"I've heard so many good things about the Wildflower Inn that I thought I'd check it out." He winked, then walked past her.

No, no, no. This wasn't a rodeo-cowboy kind of place. But short of running after him and dragging him out the front door, she couldn't do anything.

She noticed Amelia, the front-desk clerk on duty, watching her with an odd expression. "I'm heading down to the park for a few minutes." Then she made for the exit, forcing herself not to run or show any sign that anything was wrong.

She was halfway down the concrete path to the park area before she got her heartbeat under control. Logan was staying at the inn. So what? It wasn't as if she had to spend time with him. While she was friendly with all her guests, it wasn't a B and B, where a lot of interaction was expected. She'd just stick to her office and her apartment, and she'd be fine. It was only a couple more days until the rodeo, and then he'd be gone and her world would snap back to normal.

When she reached the park area, she walked to the edge of the water, closed her eyes and raised her face to the sun. She let the lapping of the water on the shore soothe her frazzled nerves. It reminded her of when she'd spent one of her spring breaks from college at the home of her roommate, Tara, in the mountains of northeast Alabama. Tara's family's property had a creek on it, and Skyler had spent an entire afternoon sitting beside it, listening to the water burbling over the rocks, letting it soothe her wounded heart. Breakups sucked, especially when they came the day before you were supposed to spend a week at the beach with said boyfriend.

"Looks like this place has seen better days."

The sound of Logan's voice jerked Skyler out of her memories and back to the present. She spun toward him. How had she not heard him approach?

"Are you stalking me?"

He had the nerve to grin. "Not in a restraining-order sort of way, no."

"Oh, well, I feel safer already."

Logan walked toward her, and she forced herself not to retreat. When he was a few steps away, he stopped, grinned, then looked at the empty posts where the dock had been. "I take it a flood did all this."

"Yeah." Yes, talk about the park. That would be a good neutral topic until she could make a getaway that didn't look like a getaway. "This used to be a popular canoe-launch and picnic area. We're hoping to rebuild it with the proceeds from this weekend's rodeo."

"You working on this?"

"I own the park now, so yeah."

"I'd think you'd have enough to do running the inn."

"I seem to have a problem saying no." Crap, had she just said that? By the way Logan's mouth twitched a little at the corner, she could tell his thoughts had shot right to last night, when all she'd seemed to be able to say was yes.

Instead of jumping on that opening, however, he turned to take in the rest of the park. "How far does the park property go?"

She pointed farther up the shore. "To where those trees are at the curve in the shoreline."

"You've got a lot of room, then."

"Yeah, I've mapped out several ideas."

He turned back toward her. "Such as?"

Why did he even care? He wasn't from Blue Falls, and come Sunday this town, this park and she would all be miles away in his rearview mirror.

"Rebuild the dock, add a canoe rental for people who don't have their own, new picnic shelters and grills, basketball and volleyball courts, a snack stand." She didn't know why she was telling him all this. Well, other than the fact that he'd asked and there was no reason not to.

"You like planning stuff, don't you?"

"Why do you say that?"

He shrugged. "The look in your eyes just now. Like you were more excited with each thing you said."

That was a little too perceptive to be comfortable. "Things need to be done, and I do them." Some would say she paid too much attention to detail, but she didn't agree with them. How could something that gave her peace be wrong?

She glanced out across the water and noticed the *Lady Fleur* paddle-wheeler taking its midday cruise.

"It seems you've got your work cut out for you," Logan said.

"It'll get done eventually. Will have to go in stages."

"You never know. We might rake in a lot of dough for you this weekend."

She smiled a little at that before she realized what she was doing. "I'll be happy if we make enough to do the cleanup and rebuild the dock."

"I'll put out the word to some friends, drum up some business for the rodeo."

She met his eyes. "Why would you do that?"

"Because I want to."

"But why? You have no stake in this."

"I don't have to have a stake in something to think it's worthwhile, do I?"

"I guess not."

"Plus, maybe I'm trying to impress you."

Her insides fluttered a little at the way he was looking at her, as though he was remembering the taste and feel of her. She had to set him straight for good.

"Listen, I don't want you to get the wrong idea because of last night. I'm not that kind of woman."

"What kind is that?"

"One who just jumps into bed with a stranger."

"I never said you were. In fact, I'm pretty sure you're the exact opposite of that."

Why did his words sting? Did he think she was as big of a fuddy-duddy as her friends did?

"So I was a challenge for you, then?"

"Yes."

Heat flooded her face.

Logan held up his hand, palm toward her. "Don't get the wrong idea."

"Why do you think I'm getting the wrong idea?"

"Maybe the look on your face that says you'd like to knee me in a tender place."

She lifted an eyebrow as if that wasn't a half-bad idea.

"I think anything worth having should be a challenge," he said.

Part of her wanted to admire that outlook on life, and maybe she would if he didn't unsettle her so much. She didn't like things that turned her life on its head. She'd had plenty of that with her dad's comings and goings. A nice calm, orderly life, that's what she wanted. That kind of life didn't include a carefree cowboy who jumped out of airplanes and had near-death experiences.

"Logan, I'm not blaming you for last night. I knew what I

was doing." As much as any insane person knew what they were doing. "But it was a one-time thing."

"I seem to remember it happening twice."

"You are being deliberately irritating."

"I like to think of it as charming."

"I think you need to look that word up in the dictionary."

He took a few steps toward her, and this time she took an involuntary step back.

"Do I make you nervous, Skyler?"

Yes. "No. I just like my personal space."

"You didn't seem to mind sharing your personal space with me last night."

She crossed her arms and stood her ground. "I can assure you that won't be happening again."

"Are you sure about that?"

"Yes."

"Why?"

Because she was afraid it would be way too easy to spend days in bed with him.

"I don't have to have a reason."

"I think it's because you liked it and wouldn't mind a repeat."

She exhaled a huff of frustration. "Talking with you is like watching a dog chase its tail."

"Only I catch what I'm after."

She rolled her eyes and turned to walk back up the path to the inn.

"Have dinner with me tonight," Logan said.

"No."

"You like me, Skyler Harrington. Admit it."

She ignored him as she kept walking.

"I don't give up easily," he called after her. "I'm going to win you over."

That was exactly what she was afraid of.

Chapter Six

Logan picked himself up out of the dirt and eyed the practice bull that had just bucked him off in two seconds flat. "We're going to have words."

"Little off your game today," Liam said from where he stood on the other side of the fence, his arms and one foot propped on the slats.

Logan climbed up the fence while the bull was directed out of the arena. "It's more that animal's nasty attitude."

"I've seen you ride way nastier than Kudzu."

Liam was right; he wasn't at his best today. He'd chalk it up to just having an off day, but he knew better. It probably wasn't good for his longevity to be thinking about a woman right before he plunked himself down on fifteen hundred pounds of bad attitude. But that was exactly what he'd done. Ever since Skyler had walked away from him earlier, he'd been devising a dozen different ways to change her attitude toward him, without an obvious winner.

"Better get your head on straight before you ride again," Liam said, sounding as though he knew exactly what had been flying around in Logan's mind. "I don't think the good folks of Blue Falls are paying to witness a cowboy kabob."

The scar on Logan's chest ached at the image. He might enjoy the thrill of riding bulls, but he wasn't crazy enough to think he was immortal. The night he'd gotten that scar was as close as he'd ever come to walking away from riding. Only the idea of his parents telling him he needed to settle down and get a real job got him through the healing and regaining his strength. The only thing scarier than getting ripped open by a bull's horn was a life of mind-numbing boredom.

After Liam walked away to deal with some managerial issue, Logan dropped to the outside of the fence and watched a couple more riders take their practice rides. When the bull riders gave way to the roping teams, he headed for his truck.

He needed to take a shower before he saw Skyler again. He didn't think she was the type of woman who found sweaty and dirty attractive. But who knew? She wasn't a one-night-stand kind of woman either, but she seemed determined that that's all they would have. So if she saw him strolling through the lobby and couldn't control herself, he had no problem giving her all the dirty, sweaty cowboy she wanted.

As he rounded a curve near the inn and glanced at the park where they'd talked earlier, he had an idea that just might help him get on her good side.

Why was he trying so dang hard with her?

Because that was the best sex he'd had in ages, and it seemed a waste for them to sleep under the same roof but in different rooms when they'd both had such a good time the night before.

He made the turn into the park and then backed the truck up to the pile of discarded lumber that had once been the dock. He pulled on his gloves and started tossing the bowed and broken wood into the bed of his truck, careful not to poke himself with any protruding nails. He figured when he had it loaded, his cousin could tell him where he could dispose of it.

Halfway through loading his truck, he looked up to see Skyler hurrying down the path from the inn.

"Miss me?" he asked when she got close enough to hear him.

"What are you doing?"

"I'd think that was obvious."

"Don't try to be cute."

"You think I'm cute?"

"Oh, my God. You're impossible. Stop right now."

He did as she commanded and leaned one hand against the side of his truck. "You said you needed this cleaned up."

"Yes, but by professionals who I pay."

"So you'd rather be out that money you could use for something else than accept my free labor."

"What if you get hurt?"

"I'm not going to sue you, if that's what you're worried about. And I ride bulls for a living. I think I can dispose of some lumber without mortal injury."

"I can't pay you."

She was really pulling out all the stops to get rid of him. He chuckled to himself. Little did she know the more she tried to give him the boot, the more determined he became to not let her.

"Did I ask for payment?"

She gave him a suspicious look, one that telegraphed exactly what she feared.

"And I'm not that kind of guy. When you end up in my bed again, it'll be because you want to be there, not because I hauled off some rotting lumber."

She crossed her arms. "When?"

He gave her a smile. "I'm ever the optimist." With that he went back to loading lumber and imagining the two of them in that big fluffy bed at the top of the hill.

A PART OF Skyler wanted to stomp her foot and scream. She was used to being able to orchestrate every aspect of her life, and Logan Bradshaw was playing havoc with that. But it wasn't as if she could physically stop him from loading the lumber. Left with either leaving or watching the muscles in his arms as he worked, she spun on her heel and headed back up to the inn.

As she walked into the lobby, she found Amelia watching Logan. "Did you hire someone to start working on the park?"

"No." She didn't elaborate at first, but when Amelia gave her a questioning look, she felt she had to. Skyler threw her hand out in Logan's direction. "It's one of the rodeo riders. Evidently, he's bored."

"The guy who checked in earlier?"

Skyler glanced back toward where Logan was close to getting all the dock lumber in his truck. "Yeah."

"Do you know him?"

"Just met yesterday." Jumped out of a plane together, danced together and, oh yeah, had hot, hot sex until the wee hours. She really had misplaced her brain yesterday.

"He sure isn't hard on the eyes."

A zing of jealousy caught Skyler unaware. Looked like maybe her insanity was leaking over into today because she had absolutely no reason to be jealous of Amelia or her appreciation of Logan's looks. Given half a chance, he'd probably take Amelia up on her interest. Skyler ground her teeth at the thought of that happening here in the inn, the place she called home. Why couldn't he have just stayed at the Country Vista?

"I'll be in my office if you need me."

"Okay," Amelia said without taking her gaze away from Logan.

Frustrated to her wits' end, Skyler turned and headed for her office. It took all of her willpower not to turn around and look out the window behind her, the window that would give her an unobstructed view of the hottest, most crazy-making guy she'd ever met.

LOGAN TOOK OFF his hat and wiped the sweat from his forehead as he eyed the second load of junk he'd delivered to the county's refuse center. He checked the sun's location and figured he had time for one more load, which would pretty much clear away the damaged materials from the park.

With a wave to the guy on duty, Logan slid into the driver's side and took off. He'd have to hurry to get the last load back here before closing.

When he pulled into the park, he noticed someone piling up the remaining debris. It wasn't until he reached the parking area that the person looked toward him and he realized it was Skyler. Gone were the professional slacks, blouse and heels from earlier. She'd changed into jeans, a T-shirt that showed off her figure quite nicely and a ball cap with her red hair pulled out the back in a ponytail.

He smiled as he got out of the truck. "I knew you couldn't resist me."

"Has anyone ever told you that you're full of yourself?"

"Often."

She tossed a big piece of driftwood onto the pile, then placed her gloved hands on her hips as she looked at him. "And that doesn't bother you?"

"Why should it? The people who say it are usually just trying to convince themselves that I'm not irresistible."

She snorted and turned to pick up some more wood and a couple of soda bottles that had washed ashore.

"Aw, come on, admit it. I'm a fun guy to be around."

"I guess you're okay sometimes."

He smiled wide, way more happy at that one little sliver of success than he should have been. He wasn't sure what it was about Skyler that made him determined to feel her next to him again. After all, she was stubborn, prickly, adamant about keeping him at more than arm's length. Was he attracted to her for no more reason than she was a challenge when he normally didn't have to work that hard with a woman?

Something about that didn't ring true. Even if Skyler Harrington wasn't so resistant to their mutual attraction, he'd still want her in his bed, tangled in his sheets with all that awesome red hair mussed about her face. Damn if he didn't get aroused just thinking about that.

One step at a time. First step was she'd actually placed herself here where she'd have to interact with him. So he started loading the truck with the material she'd collected. They didn't talk, but that was okay. He was having a nice time just appreciating how her jeans cupped her behind. But the way that red T-shirt seemed to be caressing her breasts just might do him in. He had to fight the fantasy of backing her up against the side of his truck and taking her right there.

He shook his head at the image. His body might like that idea, but Skyler wasn't that kind of woman. She was classy, professional, not a buckle chaser who would do it anywhere, anytime. For the first time in his life, the fact that he'd had sex with more than one of those women made him uncomfortable.

"You okay?"

He glanced at her, surprised by her question. "Yeah, why?"

She gestured toward him. "Your forehead was so furrowed you could have planted crops there."

"Just wondering which bull I'll draw," he said. The words were out of his mouth before he realized he'd made the decision to lie to her, to not take the opening to flirt some more. He heaved a large piece of driftwood into the truck.

"Why do you do all these dangerous things? Jumping out of airplanes, riding bulls."

"Easily bored, I guess."

He looked at her just as her expression changed. It was almost as if a dark curtain had descended over her face.

"Nothing worse than boredom."

There was an undercurrent of hostility in her tone, and for the life of him he couldn't figure out why. Despite her words,

Skyler sounded as if she could think of dozens of things that were worse than boredom.

As they tossed the last of the load into the truck, Logan closed the tailgate, then leaned back against it. "Why do you dislike me so much?"

Skyler didn't answer at first. Instead, she took off her gloves slowly and beat them against her jeans. "I don't dislike you."

"Are you sure about that?"

"I just don't want you getting the wrong idea."

"You're not the one-night-stand kind of gal. I got it."

"But it can't happen again. And you coming to stay at the inn, the continuous flirting, they all point toward you thinking that it will."

"Would that be such a bad thing?"

"Yes."

Damn if her answer didn't punch him in the gut. Maybe all this time it hadn't been that she was nervous about letting herself go. Maybe Skyler Harrington just thought she was too good for him. Well, then, good to know so he could direct his attention elsewhere.

He headed for the cab of the truck.

"Wait, Logan. I didn't mean to insult you."

"You didn't, babe. I'm just not your cup of tea." He opened the driver's-side door. "Gotta get this dumped before they close."

What he really wanted was to get as far away from Skyler as possible. As he drove toward the refuse center, he wondered why anything she'd said had upset him. But it had.

SKYLER FELT LIKE a shrew as she watched Logan drive away. He'd spent his entire afternoon cleaning up the park with no expectation of payment, and she'd repaid him by insulting him. Yes, he'd probably hauled away all the storm detritus hoping she would invite him into her bed, but he'd still done it. What was wrong with her? Was she so afraid of her own weakness that her only defense was being a bitch?

She sighed and trudged her way back up the hill, the afternoon heat baking her. She'd be lucky if she hadn't sweated off all her sunscreen and didn't look like a tomato in a few hours.

Amelia was headed out the door on her way home as Skyler reached the front of the inn. "Hon, you look like someone just pulled you out of the oven."

"I feel like it, too. There is a nice long shower in my immediate future."

Amelia looked past her toward the park. "It looks a lot better."

Skyler turned to look at the park and had to agree. With all the storm damage removed, she was able to see her plans for the park more clearly. And that was thanks to Logan Bradshaw. She needed to apologize to him. Just because she'd made an error in judgment didn't give her the right to act the way she had. He was what he was, an incurable flirt. She didn't have to be rude in order to get the message across that his flirtations weren't going to work a second time. Well, third if you wanted to be precise about it.

After she finished showering and getting dressed, she looked up what room Logan was staying in and called him. There wasn't an answer, so she went back into the hotel's computer system and made a note that he was to have a free dinner and breakfast at the inn's dining room. It wasn't much in repayment for the work he'd done, but at least it was something. She'd stepped away from the computer when she had another thought. She sat back down and comped his room for the two nights he'd booked, as well. She felt better after that, though she still needed to apologize for her rudeness. That proved impossible when he continued to not answer his phone. More curious than she should be, she walked outside around midnight to find his truck still not in the parking lot.

Something unpleasant squeezed inside her at the thought that she'd finally gotten her message of noninterest across and Logan had found some other honey to occupy his time. She should be happy that she wouldn't have to deal with his overwhelming attention anymore, but for some reason she wasn't. As she lay in her bed, it had never seemed so big and empty.

SKYLER GOT UP the next morning determined to not have her day's thoughts center around a certain cowboy. That proved difficult, however, when she walked down Main Street and saw posters for that night's rodeo in every store window and stapled to several utility poles. And as if that wasn't bad enough, the cowboy featured riding an enormous bull was none other than Logan.

Her cheeks flamed when she remembered how those legs gripping that bull had felt when they were rubbing against hers. Shaking her head, she walked the rest of the way to Yesterwear, India's vintage-inspired shop. When she stepped inside, the front counter was manned by Lara, India's teenage summer employee.

"Hey, Skyler. India and Elissa are next door."

"Thanks." As Skyler walked through the store, a new outfit caught her eye. The frilly blouse and skirt had an Old West feel to it while still managing to be modern. India had such a good eye for that kind of thing.

When she stepped through the new doorway that led into the adjoining building, she spotted her friends talking to Liam and Len Goodall, who was handling the conversion of the formerly empty building into extra space for Yesterwear.

She realized she hadn't seen or talked to Elissa since she'd left Skyler's office without a word. But when Elissa spotted her, she smiled and waved. Skyler exhaled in relief, glad her friend got over being upset so quickly. Elissa wasn't the type of person to let anything keep her in a bad mood for long.

"It's looking good," Skyler said as she approached the group. Already the quarter-circle stage was coming together in the back corner, as was the framework for three dressing rooms adjacent to the stage.

India's face glowed with happiness. Not only had Liam proved to be the love of her life, but his buying the building was allowing her to fulfill her dream of expanding her business. Liam was quite a catch, and a little part of Skyler was jealous. She didn't begrudge India any of her good fortune, but she couldn't help thinking about what it would be like to find that kind of love herself. Her thoughts went back to her night with Logan until she forcibly pushed them away.

"So is this why we're here?" Skyler asked. "You were a bit on the vague side when you called."

"Oh, no." India motioned for Skyler and Elissa to follow her. Instead of heading for the front of the store, she veered toward the storage room. Once inside, she placed her hands down across three identical boxes. "I got us something to wear to the rodeo tonight. Consider it a little thank-you for getting Liam and me together."

"You didn't have to get us presents," Skyler said.

"Speak for yourself, missy." Elissa rubbed her hands together. "I love presents, and I worked danged hard for this one."

The three of them laughed.

India flipped off the boxes' lids in quick succession to reveal three pairs of colorful cowgirl boots.

"These are awesome!" Elissa picked up a purple pair covered with scrollwork and hand-tooled flowers.

"These are for you," India said to Skyler as she indicated a pair of aqua boots with dark blue flowers and stitching.

"You didn't have to do this. I wasn't half as pushy as Elissa."

"Hey," Elissa said in mock offense. "Wait. You're right."

Skyler nodded toward the remaining pair of boots, which were obviously India's. "The red ones are perfect for you."

"So, Skyler, when we finally get your guy snagged, I'd like to request a spa day for my thank-you gift."

Skyler couldn't even be mad at Elissa. She came by her annoying matchmaking genes naturally. After all, her aunt Verona didn't hold the title of Blue Falls' cupid for nothing. "You're going to be waiting awhile."

"Really? From what I hear, you and the luscious Logan were working together to clean up the park yesterday."

"Yes, and filling a truck with driftwood and trash is so incredibly romantic."

"Honey, anything can be romantic if you work it right."

"I know you're trying to help in your own crazy way, but Logan Bradshaw was a one-time thing. He'll be gone tomorrow, and hopefully he'll take my temporary insanity with him."

"I personally think you would have been insane if you hadn't jumped his bones," Elissa said as she put her purple boot back in the box.

Skyler ignored her.

They talked a couple more minutes before Skyler said she needed to get back to the inn to get some more work done before she headed over to the rodeo.

"We'll save you a good seat," Elissa said. "You need to have a clear view of Logan's attributes."

"Keep it up and I'll tell Bernie Shumaker you've got the hots for him." Bernie was the local jack-of-all-trades but master of none. No one knew how old he was, but ancient would suffice as a guess.

"Make sure his hearing aid is turned up or he won't hear you."

Skyler shook her head and left. But once outside, she

headed for the Mehlerhaus Bakery across the street instead of her car.

"Hey, Skyler," Keri Teague, the bakery's owner, said as she looked up from where she was decorating a cake. "What can I get for you today?"

When Skyler looked at the display case, she noticed one of the rodeo posters taped to the front of the glass. Drat, the man was everywhere. "I'll take a dozen of the lemon cookies and another dozen of the oatmeal-raisin." One of the perks she offered her inn guests, fresh cookies from the bakery.

Her gaze kept going back to the poster despite her best intentions.

"That's the guy you were dancing with the other night, isn't it?"

Skyler jerked her attention to Keri, who now stood on the other side of the display case and had obviously caught her gawking. "Yeah."

"I have to say these rodeos are bringing some mighty fine–looking men to town."

"You tell Simon that?"

"As a matter of fact, I did."

Skyler laughed a little. "I'm sure he liked that."

"He might have reminded me why I chose to marry him." Keri winked. "And that might have been my plan all along."

For the second time in the past few minutes, Skyler felt a pang of longing in her middle when she thought about the happiness her friends had found in the most unexpected places.

But that didn't mean she was going to find her own happily-ever-after with someone like Logan.

"Go ahead and give me another one of those lemon cookies," she said before Keri closed the sliding glass door on the display case.

She paid, accepted her purchases and headed out the bakery's door. The cookie was nothing more than a memory by the time she reached her car. Before she reached the inn, two more had followed it. Self-pity wasn't attractive. And it was fattening.

Chapter Seven

Skyler left her apartment determined to not feel sorry for herself anymore. She had no reason to. After all, she had a great life—a successful business, awesome friends, a wonderful community. And after tonight she'd even be able to start work on the rebuilding of the park.

Thanks to Logan.

She shook her head as she got in her car, but it didn't work in dislodging the image of Logan as he worked on clearing debris from the park. He'd been dirty, sweaty and probably stinky, too, but he'd also been sexy as hell. The man did very nice things for jeans and T-shirts.

Or no clothing at all.

Good grief, you'd think she was an infatuated teenager lusting after the captain of the football team.

When she reached the fairgrounds, she headed straight for the lemonade stand. As she expected, the line was long. But there was nothing better to beat the July heat than the fresh-squeezed lemonade made by the football boosters. When she finally reached the front of the line, she bought the largest lemonade they had. But as she headed toward the grandstand, a couple of kids ran out from between two parked horse trailers and slammed into her. She gasped as the contents of her cup spilled right down the front of her shirt.

The kids, sensing they were about to get yelled at, took off at a dead run before she could even tell who they were.

"I didn't know there was going to be a wet T-shirt contest tonight."

She looked up to see a couple of cowboys watching her just as the one who hadn't spoken whistled at her. When someone's hands clasped her shoulders, she yelped and spun away. It took a moment for her to realize it was Logan. He gave the other two cowboys a hard stare, then moved so that he was shielding her from them.

"Come on." He placed his hand on her back and guided her toward where several RVs were parked.

"Where are we going?"

"To get you a clean shirt."

She stopped. "I have more shirts."

Logan turned to face her. "With you?"

"No, but I can run home."

"You've already paid to get in. There's no sense in you leaving when I've got something you can use."

She started to protest again but stopped herself before she voiced the words. "I'm sorry."

"For what?"

"How rude I've been to you."

He shrugged. "I'm sorry if I was too pushy. Now, are you going to let me save the day or not?"

She smiled a little at that. If she were a different kind of woman, she could easily fall under his very tempting spell. But she was strong enough to accept his help without giving in to temptation again.

He led her through the maze of RVs until they reached his truck.

"Aren't all your things in your room?"

"I always keep a few things in the truck in case I need them."

She couldn't help but wonder if that was because sometimes he didn't end up making it back to his own room.

He retrieved a small gym bag from the truck and pulled a green T-shirt out. "It'll be big on you, but at least it won't be plastered to you like a second skin."

Suddenly self-conscious, she crossed her arms over her breasts.

Logan leaned close. "I've already seen them."

She flushed at the memory of his mouth capturing her breasts. Needing to get away from him, she took the proffered shirt and turned to leave.

"Where are you going?"

"To the bathroom to change."

"You'll have to walk past half the people here to get to the bathroom. Just change here. No one's nearby."

"You're here."

"I'll turn my back."

"I'm not sure I trust you."

He made an X over his heart. "Cross my heart and hope to die."

A jolt of fear went through her. "Don't say that."

He gave her a confused look.

"You're about to ride an animal with ginormous horns. Don't tempt fate."

"Why, Miss Harrington, you almost sound like you care."

"Don't flatter yourself. I don't want to see anyone get hurt."

"Mmm-hmm," he said, obviously sticking with his idea that she cared about his welfare specifically.

"Oh, turn around."

He laughed as he complied. "If you need any help, just let me know."

"Amazingly, I've been dressing myself for nearly thirty years."

"Just trying to be neighborly."

She snorted at that. Then, with a quick glance to make sure he wasn't peeking, she swapped her wet shirt for his dry one. There was nothing she could do about the wet bra. That was going to be sticky and uncomfortable, but if Logan had a bra in his truck, she certainly didn't want it.

He turned toward her. "See, I'm useful for something besides hauling lumber and being a flirt."

"Thank you."

"How about you give me a good-luck kiss instead?" He leaned toward her with puckered lips, causing her to laugh.

She stepped out of reach. "Good luck with your ride."

He made an exaggerated pout, which made her smile all the way back to her car to toss her wet shirt inside.

The opening ceremony was already under way by the time she reached the grandstand and found her friends.

Elissa gave her a questioning look as Skyler sat down on the end of the bleacher. "Where did that T-shirt come from? And why do you smell like lemonade?"

She was saved from answering by the call to stand for the playing of the national anthem. But Elissa wasn't so easily deterred. As soon as the song was over and they sat again, she said, "Well?"

"Couple of kids ran into me, and I got lemonade all over my shirt."

"And you just happened to have a shirt that's several sizes too large with you?"

"I borrowed it, okay?"

Elissa finally shut up, but Skyler wasn't sure the knowing smirk she wore wasn't more irritating than the questions.

As one event after another passed, Skyler tried not to make eye contact with Elissa. Instead, she talked to India about a new designer she'd found, chitchatted with Keri and the rest of the Teague clan, and watched Liam's daughter, Ginny, chatting with her bestie, Mia Monroe.

"I'm surprised Jake brought Mia out tonight." Skyler kept her voice low so Mia's dad couldn't hear her.

"He says it's better for her to get out and see people, do things," India said. "She gets depressed when he keeps her at home."

"How much more treatment does she have?"

"Eight weeks, I think."

The cost of Mia's cancer treatments had been the catalyst for the first of the benefit rodeos. Part of Skyler wanted to hand over any proceeds from tonight's event, as well, but the city and Liam's rodeo company had set up the future events so that no one cause benefited from more than one rodeo. That would ensure fairness and the ability to spread the wealth around.

The public-address announcer told the crowd that the bull riding was up next, and Skyler's nerves sparked to life. Logan might not be the man for her, but she certainly didn't want him injured. She couldn't get the sight of that jagged scar on his chest out of her mind as she watched one cowboy after another go flying through the air.

"Next up we've got a first-timer here at Blue Falls, but he's had plenty of bull-riding experience. Logan Bradshaw will be riding Smokin' Joe."

Skyler held her breath as she saw Logan settle himself astride the bull and nod that he was ready. In a blink, the bull and Logan were out in the arena, the bull trying its best to rid itself of the man on its back.

"I think they should have named that one Jumpin' Joe," Simon Teague said from the next bleacher up.

Eight seconds had never lasted so long. Only when Logan had climbed out of the danger zone did she breathe more easily.

Elissa nudged her shoulder. "Your boy did good. Might just win this thing."

Skyler fought the urge to leave, to go back to the calm and quiet of her apartment, where there was no danger of watching someone be gored to death. Somehow she made it through the rest of the bull riding and a couple more teasing remarks from Elissa, even a knowing grin from India. Once the rodeo was over, she slid off the bleachers.

"See you at the music hall," Elissa said.

"I'm headed home. I'm beat."

Elissa started to say something else, but India grabbed her arm and clapped her hand over Elissa's mouth as she guided her away. Skyler mouthed a "thank you" when India glanced back at her.

As she drove through town and saw the crowd gathering at the music hall, she almost changed her mind. Just because her last time there had led to her going back to Logan's motel didn't mean that would happen again. She wasn't completely without restraint.

Or was she?

Just to be on the safe side, she drove the rest of the way home, took a shower and washed a load of laundry, including her sticky shirt and bra and the T-shirt she'd borrowed from Logan. She'd leave it in an envelope for him at the front desk to pick up when he checked out in the morning. Maybe she wouldn't even have to see him before he left town. Part of her didn't like that idea, but the part that had some sense knew it was the best thing. He wasn't a staying kind of guy, and that's what she needed if she decided to take that kind of chance.

When her phone received a text, she almost didn't look at it in case it was Elissa bugging her to come to the music hall. But it was actually from Liam telling her how much they'd made on the rodeo. It was a good amount, enough to get the dock rebuilt and the picnic shelters filled with new tables. But the rest of her plans were going to have to stay nothing more than ideas for the foreseeable future.

She tried reading to take her mind off of everything, but it didn't work. Neither did watching TV or making sure all of her kitchen cabinets were in perfect order. She closed the last cabinet and headed for her office. When she stepped out of her apartment, she heard laughter coming from the dining room at the far end of the hallway on the other side of the lobby. Some of the guests were evidently eating a late dinner. She was glad to hear they were having a good time, but something about the sound of their laughter made her feel even more alone than she had inside her apartment.

She took a deep breath and opened her office door. Once inside, she started some melodic Celtic music playing and pulled out her plans for the park. She wasn't sure when she'd become so attached to the ideas sketched out in front of her, but she had. She hated not having the means to put her plans in motion, but it wouldn't be the first time she'd had to be patient to get what she wanted. As she'd been saving up enough money for a down payment on the inn, she had lived in fear that the previous owners would back out on their promise to wait for her. It had seemed to take forever, but she'd done it.

There was another way to get the money, but that might never come to pass.

"You're working late."

She jumped at the sound of Logan's voice. He stood in the doorway, all long, tall, handsome-as-sin cowboy.

"I get more done when the phone isn't ringing."

"Good thing about riding bulls. Nobody calls me when I'm working."

"But then, I don't have to worry about my office stabbing me to death."

"I don't know. I hear letter openers can be sneaky devils."

She shook her head. "I figured you'd be burning up the dance floor at the music hall with everyone else in town."

"I went for a little bit, but my favorite dance partner wasn't there."

"I think I need a pair of waders. It's getting deep in here."

"You don't take compliments very well," he said.

"I might accept it if I thought you meant it."

"I do."

She looked up at him and was tempted to believe him. Maybe a part of him even did mean it. After all, she'd never doubted her father's love for her mother. And when he promised to "stay this time," he might have even believed what he was saying. But the allure of the new and exciting always pulled him away, and Logan Bradshaw was cut from the same cloth.

Logan gestured toward the top of her desk. "What are you working on?"

"Plans for the park."

"Can I see?"

"Sure." What could it possibly hurt to show him? She spun the drawing around so he could see.

It took Logan only a couple of steps to cross to her desk, and the moment he was in the room he seemed to fill it. As he leaned forward to look at her sketch, she'd swear she could smell him, an oddly alluring mixture of earth and man. For a crazy moment, she imagined sweeping everything off her desk and letting him take her on top of it.

Skyler leaned back in her chair, putting distance between them. She needed this man to leave Blue Falls and quickly. He made her feel and think things that were so unlike herself that they left her jittery.

"Looks like a big project."

"Yeah. Realistically, it might never happen, but at least we can restore it to what it was before."

Logan sank into one of the chairs opposite her. "You seem

like a pretty determined woman. I'd lay money on you making it happen."

"Unless someone gives me a money tree or you know someone who'd like to buy a run-down ranch, then I wouldn't place that bet if I were you."

"A ranch?"

Why had she even mentioned that? Because she didn't really have a good reason for not elaborating.

"A family ranch. I've been trying to sell it for years, but no takers. Of course, it needs some work done."

"Ranching is hard work."

"I know." It didn't help that it had been neglected since her mother's death, and Skyler couldn't bring herself to even attempt to fix it up. Every time she'd thought about it and driven out there, she'd been overwhelmed and not even gotten out of her car.

Logan gestured toward the sketch. "Maybe you get all of that up and running, and you'll make enough off the canoe rentals and the concessions to fix up the ranch and make it more attractive to buyers."

She was shaking her head even before he finished. "I can't even think about that right now. I already feel like I'm juggling knives and I'm made out of balloons sometimes."

Why was she telling him all this? Maybe it was because he'd be gone tomorrow. The fact that he was leaving in the morning reminded her of his shirt. She rolled her chair back and stood.

"Going somewhere?"

"To get your shirt." She hurried into her apartment to retrieve the shirt, but he didn't stay in her office. Instead, she found him standing right outside her door. She extended the folded shirt to put a barrier between them.

"You know, you should keep it," he said, the sound of his voice rumbling deep inside her, making her flirt with the idea of pulling him into her apartment. "It looks better on you, anyway."

"No, I have plenty of T-shirts, thanks."

He lifted the shirt to his nose. "You washed it?"

"Yeah, I wasn't going to give you a dirty shirt back."

He smiled. "I doubt you got it very dirty in the few hours you wore it." He rubbed his thumb across the soft fabric. "Though I'm glad you did. Now it will smell like you."

"Logan." She tried to back up but her door had closed behind her.

"Skyler, this doesn't have to be a big deal. We're both adults, ones with needs."

"Yes, and I need to go to bed."

"Exactly what I had in mind."

"Alone."

Logan sighed, then cupped her jaw. Her breath caught as his lips descended toward hers. She should push him away, but she couldn't move her hands. His kiss was sweet, gentle. Final. When he pulled back, he ran his thumb over her lips.

"It was nice knowing you, Skyler Harrington."

Skyler watched him turn and walk away, part of her screaming to stop him, to indulge in one more night with this man before he was gone from her life forever. But she stayed quiet, frozen in place, until he walked through the door to the stairs leading to the second floor.

She lifted her fingertips to her lips and touched them, imagining she could still feel the warmth of him. A warmth she had the horrible feeling it was going to take a long time to forget.

LOGAN SHOWERED THE familiar smells of rodeo down the drain of the large tile shower. There was plenty of room in the shower for two people, and he hardened at the idea of Skyler in here with him. He'd seen the desire in her eyes, the desire she didn't want to give in to again.

He turned off the shower and dried himself before wrapping a towel around his waist and walking into the bedroom. He stretched out on the bed and flicked on the TV. After making two complete circuits through the channels without anything that captured his interest, he turned it off and tossed the remote to the other side of the king-size bed. He lay staring at the ceiling, listening to occasional footsteps approaching and then passing his door.

He glanced at the clock and accepted that Skyler wasn't going to be joining him. Part of him thought maybe he should have stayed at the music hall a bit longer, but that oddly didn't hold any appeal. No, he'd just get a good night's rest and hit the road to Tulsa early in the morning.

Normally, he slept like a log after a rodeo unless he was hurt. When he woke a little before six after only sporadic sleep and more tossing and turning than a ship in rough seas, he gave up trying and got up. Time to move on, to leave behind Blue Falls and whatever number Skyler Harrington had done to his head.

Chapter Eight

"It's looking good, Len," Skyler said as she examined the nearly completed dock, including a new attendant hut at the end for when she got the canoe rental up and going.

"Yeah, we'll be done by the end of the day."

"When you finish, come up to the inn and dinner's on me."

She left Len and his teenage son to their work and headed back up the hill. Already the heat was approaching Hades level. She was exhausted from it halfway up the hill. She wanted to kiss her air conditioner the moment she stepped into the lobby.

"Going to be another scorcher," Amelia said. "It's already ninety-six."

"Sometimes I wonder how we don't all melt into a puddle of goo."

She headed for the dining area and found Elissa and India already there drinking coffee. It was time to plan the next BlueBelles enrichment class for young girls, their combined contribution back to the community that had elected them the Belle of Blue Falls during their high school days, the three of them holding the title one after another for three consecutive years.

Skyler poured her own cup and grabbed a bran muffin from the buffet. As she turned toward the table, her head spun and she had to reach out to steady herself on the back of a chair.

India noticed and started to stand before Skyler waved her off.

"Are you okay?" India asked as Skyler reached the table and took her seat.

"Fine. Just the blasted heat. What I wouldn't give for some rain." She grabbed a glass of water off the table and pressed it against her forehead.

"Your face is almost as red as your hair," Elissa said.

"Just call me Lobster Girl."

They dived into planning their next class, but Skyler had trouble paying attention when her stomach started rolling.

"Are you sure you're okay, Skyler?" India pressed the back of her hand against Skyler's forehead. "You don't feel any warmer than normal."

"I don't know. I don't feel very good." The words were barely out of her mouth before her stomach really started doing somersaults. She jumped up from the table and hurried down the hall to her apartment. She barely made it to the bathroom before she threw up.

Suddenly, her friends were there with her, holding her hair out of the way and rubbing her back. When she was finally through retching, she sat and leaned against the wall. Elissa handed her a wet cloth so she could wipe her mouth.

"Did you eat anything weird last night?" India asked.

"No. I guess I could have picked up a bug from one of the guests, though I don't remember anyone being sick."

"Well, I think you need to take the day off. You work all the time, anyway."

Skyler smiled at India. "Sure you're not talking about yourself?"

"I take off more time than I used to."

"Gotta keep that hot cowboy happy," Elissa teased.

Elissa's comment sent Skyler right back to the night she'd spent with Logan. The longer he was gone, the easier it got to not think about him. The question that wouldn't stop plaguing her was why she thought about him at all. It wasn't as if he was the only guy she'd ever had sex with.

When she looked up, relegating her thoughts to the past where they belonged, Elissa had a strange expression on her face.

"What?"

"Could you be pregnant?"

"What? No!"

"Are you sure?"

"We only had sex twice, and we used protection both times."

"Any chance the protection failed?"

"No." She paused, thinking back to that night. "I don't think so." She would have noticed something like that and started freaking out immediately instead of now, three weeks later. This couldn't be happening.

India took her hand between hers. "Don't panic yet. It may be nothing more than a stomach bug."

Please, let that be it. That she could get past in a few days. A kid? That was a forever kind of thing.

"Come on," India said as she helped Skyler to her feet and to the sink so she could wash out her mouth.

"I'll be back in a few minutes."

Skyler glanced up at Elissa as she headed toward the bathroom door. "Where are you going?"

"To get a pregnancy test."

"No, there's no need for that. I can't be pregnant." Maybe if she said it enough, believed it enough, she could make it reality.

"How about we make sure?"

That was actually a good idea. She could tinkle on a stick,

get the negative sign and stop panicking. Instead, she could curl up in her bed and sleep until she felt better.

As Elissa made another move to leave, Skyler grabbed her arm. "Don't tell anyone."

"I won't. I'll just pop by the clinic with a fresh bunch of flowers, wander to the back to see Chloe. She won't say a word either."

Chloe Brody grew up on the ranch just down the road from Skyler's family's ranch. Her brothers and dad still ran the ranch even though Chloe had gone to medical school before coming back to Blue Falls as a doctor.

Skyler nodded, then allowed India to help her to the bed. "I feel so weak and tired."

"That's probably your nerves more than anything."

Skyler sat on the side of the bed and started shaking her head. "I can't be pregnant. I just can't." She planned for everything, and this definitely wasn't in the plan. Well, maybe someday, but not now. She'd like to be married to someone she loved first.

Logan's image formed in her mind, and she nearly growled at it. That face was what got her into this mess.

India sat beside her and wrapped her arm around Skyler's shoulders. "Listen, you're getting ahead of yourself. You very well might not be pregnant. And if you are, you'll manage."

"How am I supposed to manage a kid? I have a business to run, projects to finish."

"Hon, single mothers manage every day."

"And some of them end up in early graves because of it." Tears pooled in her eyes at the memory of how hard her mother had worked when Skyler's dad was off on one wild-goose chase or another.

India pulled Skyler's head onto her shoulder and kissed her forehead. "You know your mom had a heart condition. It had nothing to do with taking care of you. She would have passed even if you weren't in the picture."

Skyler knew what India said was true, but she couldn't stop thinking that her mother might have lived even a little bit longer if she hadn't had so much riding on her shoulders.

"Now, why don't you rest until Elissa gets back?"

She didn't think that was possible, but she lay down, anyway. India left the room, leaving Skyler to stare at the ceiling and let questions consume her. What was she going to do if she was pregnant? When she started showing, everyone in town would know. Would it affect her business? She imagined whispered conversations at the Primrose full of speculation about the identity of the father.

Logan. She didn't even know where he was. If she was freaking out at the idea of having a child, she could only imagine what someone like him would do. He'd likely head for the farthest point on the globe from her. Which was probably the best thing. He wasn't exactly father material.

Skyler thought she might go crazy before Elissa returned from the clinic and pulled a plain white bag from her purse. It looked so ordinary, like a sack that could be filled with a school lunch. Instead, it held a little magic stick that would tell her whether she had making school lunches in her future.

She pulled herself back to the side of the bed and accepted the pregnancy test. Her hand shook as she grasped the box. When she stood, another wave of dizziness hit her. But she took a deep breath and it passed.

"Do you need help to the bathroom?" India asked.

"No, I'm fine." At least she would be the moment she saw the negative sign.

Once inside the bathroom, she sat atop the closed toilet and stared at the test. It felt as if she was about to open Pandora's box. With a deep breath, she ripped open the package and did what she needed to do.

Then the waiting began. The horrible, interminable, fate-of-her-world waiting. She stood and straightened all the toiletries on the vanity, lotions and face creams and brushes that didn't need straightening.

"You okay?" Elissa asked through the door.

"Yeah."

"Come out and have something to drink while you wait."

"I'll be out in a minute." She glanced at the clock. Actually, she wasn't leaving this room for another two and a half minutes. And if she didn't like the result of the test, she might just stay in here forever.

She moved to the towel rack and made sure the edges of the towel lined up precisely, then picked at imaginary lint. She knew what was happening. The more anxious she was, the more her tendency to fixate on everything being just so showed itself.

Another glance at the clock revealed that only twenty seconds had passed since the last time she looked. The pregnancy test sat there on the back of the toilet, mocking her with its lack of answers. By the time another minute passed, she'd decided the makers of home pregnancy tests should be flogged for inflicting cruel and unusual punishment.

She listened to someone pacing in her bedroom. It had to be India. Elissa wasn't a pacer. She was more of a "let things happen because they happen for a reason" person. Skyler couldn't imagine what reason Fate could possibly have for scaring the living daylights out of her like this. She rubbed her chest, afraid the heart disease that ran in her mother's family was about to claim another victim.

Not wanting to start pacing the confines of her bathroom, she sank onto the edge of the tub and closed her eyes. She focused on breathing slowly and deeply so she didn't pass out before she got her answer. She resorted to counting "one Mississippi, two Mississippi" in her head to help pass the time.

When she was pretty sure the full three minutes had passed, she opened her eyes and stared at the pregnancy test. Now that it probably held an answer, she was afraid to move close enough to see it.

"Skyler?" India said through the door.

She didn't respond. Instead, she stood and forced herself to look at the stick. Tears pooled in her eyes and quickly obscured the result. The door to the bathroom opened, and Skyler felt as if she was moving in slow motion as she turned toward her friends. They knew as soon as they looked at her, but she found the words tumbling from her lips, anyway.

"I'm going to have a baby."

"SUCK IT IN, sister," Elissa said as she tried to zip up Skyler's bridesmaid dress.

The moment the dress was fully zipped, Skyler turned and stared at her friend. "I think your purpose in this world is to be an ever-present thorn in my side."

Elissa had the nerve to smile. "You know you love me."

"You just told me to suck it in. I'm pregnant, not fat." It had been a week and a half since the pregnancy test followed by a quick trip to see Chloe just to make sure, and she still couldn't believe there was a tiny life growing inside her. Every morning when she woke up, she was convinced it had all been a dream. No one other than Elissa, India and Chloe knew, and Skyler intended to keep it that way until she had no choice but to tell people.

"You forget I saw you mow through half a dozen of Keri's cookies last night."

"I could do that before I got pregnant."

Elissa cocked an eyebrow at that.

"Well, I could," Skyler insisted. "Her lemon cookies are seriously addictive, and you know it."

"Whatever, chubs."

Skyler swatted Elissa with her bouquet. Elissa just laughed and moved to help India with her veil. India looked so beautiful in her bridal finery that Skyler nearly started crying. Who was she kidding? Commercials about puppy food could make her cry now. Damn hormones.

Skyler knew that Elissa's teasing was her way of trying to keep her upbeat, to prevent her from worrying every moment of every day. Everything from whether she was exercising enough or too much to the best kind of diapers to what her friends and neighbors were going to think of her plagued her nonstop. She was so anxious that Chloe had told her in no uncertain terms that she had to cut out the constant fretting.

She was trying to focus on other things, but it was easier said than done when she was packing the kidlet around with her 24/7. Add to that the fact that a month in and she was already tired, cranky, her boobs hurt and, yes, her clothes were getting a little tighter. At this rate, she was going to be enormous in no time.

She'd already caught Verona giving her a couple of suspicious looks. How long would it be before other people started noticing things were off? And what about when Jesse found out? Would he figure out it was Logan's and tell his cousin? Did she want him to? No, she couldn't think about that now.

When India turned to face them, Skyler's worries about the future faded.

"You've got to be the most beautiful bride ever." Skyler thought that the radiant smile on India's face was the most important piece of the ensemble.

"That Liam is a lucky guy," Elissa added, then kissed India on the cheek.

India took Elissa's hand in one of hers and motioned for Skyler to come forward so she could capture hers, too. When she held both of their hands, she squeezed them. "This wouldn't have happened without the two of you. I know I didn't make it easy, but I'm glad you didn't give up on me. You're the best friends a girl could ever have."

Skyler bit her lip and lifted her free hand to wipe away a tear.

"Oh, look, you made ol' Hormoney cry."

Skyler stuck out her tongue at Elissa. "Just you wait. If this kid gets colic, I'm dropping it off at Auntie Elissa's for an extended visit."

"That's okay. It's all part of my plan to secure favorite-aunt status."

"Good luck with that," India said. "Aunt India is going to have horses and a shopful of pretty clothes if it's a girl."

Elissa made a face that said she knew a plant nursery couldn't compete with that, making India and Skyler laugh.

It felt good to laugh, and Skyler made a promise to herself that for today she was going to have a good time. She owed it to India, who had waited a lifetime to be this happy and deserved to have her big day be fairy-tale perfect. Even the weather was cooperating. Overnight showers had brought cooler weather. Well, cool for Texas in early August, anyway.

"You girls sound like you're having way too much fun in here."

The three of them looked toward the door as Verona came into Skyler's apartment. She was dressed in a shimmery dark blue suit that complemented the pale blue dresses that Elissa and Skyler wore.

"How many times do I have to tell you there's no such thing as too much fun?" Elissa said.

Skyler's mind went straight to that night at the Country Vista Inn. Yes, there was such a thing as too much fun.

"You ready?" Verona asked, drawing Skyler back to the present.

India nodded. "Thank you for doing this."

"Sweetie, you've already thanked me half a dozen times."

"I know, but it means a lot to me."

Verona had agreed to walk India down the aisle since India didn't have any family. And Elissa and Skyler had made sure that India's side of the outdoor wedding space was filled with friends. Today of all days, India didn't need to think about her utter lack of family. Before the sun went down, she would have a new family—a husband, a stepdaughter and Liam's parents, who had treated India like a daughter from the moment they realized how much she meant to their son. There might not be carriages with white horses, glass slippers or a prince, but this was no less a fairy tale. Skyler's heart swelled as she watched India take Verona's arm.

"Well, girls, I think it's time to get this show on the road," Verona said.

Skyler fought tears during their walk from her apartment to the flower-filled courtyard, as India and Liam said their vows, as Ginny looked up at her dad with a smile as wide as Texas. This was right, the way things should be. When the minister finally pronounced them husband and wife and Liam planted a big cheer-inducing kiss on India, Skyler finally lost the battle and had to wipe away a tear.

"Are you okay?" Elissa whispered next to her.

"Yeah, just happy."

Her happiness for her friend didn't wane as everyone shifted into party mode. But as the sun slipped below the horizon and couples paired up for dancing, Skyler had to fight the urge to slip away. As she watched Liam and India move around the dance floor in each other's arms, she remembered watching them dance by that night at the music hall. Remembered how good it had felt to be held in Logan's arms.

"May I have this dance?"

Pete Kayne, one of Sheriff Simon Teague's deputies and all-around good guy, offered his arm.

She started to decline but then worried that people would

wonder why she wasn't dancing at her best friend's wedding. "Don't mind if I do."

But as Pete guided her through the song, Skyler couldn't stop thinking about Logan, wondering where he was. She thought about the life growing inside of her and hoped it was a girl, because she didn't know if she could handle looking into the eyes of a miniature Logan.

"You okay, Skyler?"

She jerked her attention back to Pete. "Yeah, fine."

If by fine she meant facing a pregnancy and motherhood by herself, but now wasn't the time or place to make that announcement.

Tonight was about the beginning of happily-ever-after.

LOGAN FLIPPED DOWN his truck's visor to shield his eyes from the intense glare of the setting sun. He shifted in his seat, trying to get the kinks out of his back. He'd tweaked it in last night's ride in Houston, enough that he'd pulled out of the rodeo in Albuquerque next weekend. The only bright spot was he was in Texas. Might as well visit Jesse. And if he happened to cross paths with Skyler and she'd missed him so much that she jumped his bones? Well, that would be okay, too.

He'd thought about her more than once over the past month, and at the oddest times. Most frequently it was when he was about to fall asleep, but she'd been known to enter his head as he was driving down the road or when he was in a bar and a song reminded him of her. On a couple of occasions, he'd even turned down female advances, but he'd explained that away by telling himself he was just tired. He certainly couldn't be hung up on a woman he'd known only a handful of days.

As he got close to Blue Falls, he pulled out his phone and called Jesse. He let it ring until the voice mail came on, then left Jesse a message that he was in town and would greatly appreciate a couch to crash on.

What he'd really like was one of those soft beds at the Wildflower Inn, but he thought Skyler might look at him more favorably if he didn't take up temporary residence again. Still, that didn't mean he couldn't stop by and use that free-dinner coupon that had been riding around in his wallet for a month. And if he happened to bump into Skyler, he wasn't going to complain.

Business must have been good, because the inn's parking lot was full. It sounded as if a party was going on when he got out of his truck and approached the front door. When he stepped inside, the gal at the front desk, the same one who'd checked him in before, looked up from her computer screen.

"Hello. Are you staying with us again?"

"No, just came by to have dinner."

"They've got a really good salmon special tonight."

He was more of a red-meat kind of guy, but he nodded his thanks for her suggestion, anyway. As he turned to head for the dining room, he spotted a guy in a tux coming out of the bathroom. It took him a moment to realize it was Liam.

"Nice monkey suit, man," Logan said. "What's the occasion?"

Liam tugged at his tie, finally giving in and ripping it off and stuffing it in his pocket. "It's my wedding day. Couldn't get away with jeans and boots."

"Another one ties the knot." Logan shook Liam's hand. "More ladies for me."

Liam laughed and clapped him on the shoulder, causing Logan to wince. "You injured?"

"It's nothing. Just a tweak. A bull in Houston didn't want to be friends."

"Sounds like you need a drink. Come on out to the party."

"I'm not exactly in my best duds."

"You're not the one getting married."

"Thank God for that." For some reason Skyler's image popped into his mind. He rubbed his hand over his face as he followed Liam outside and around the far corner of the building. Maybe that dang bull had shaken his brain loose just to add insult to back injury.

When he came within sight of the crowd and saw Skyler, however, he thought he might owe that wretched bull a kiss.

The woman would look good wearing a plastic garbage bag, but the blue dress that left one shoulder bare nearly had him panting. If there was a more stunning woman in the world, he'd never seen her. And if tonight went really, really well, he planned to kiss that bare shoulder and maybe a lot more.

Chapter Nine

Skyler laughed right along with everyone else when Simon Teague finished telling the story about rolling up to Frank Pepperdine's junkyard to find Pete standing on top of his patrol car trying to get Frank's Rottweiler to stop growling at him.

"If I hadn't yelled at Frank that I was going to lock him up for a month for assaulting an officer, Pete would still be standing up there."

"I would have liked to see you do any different if you'd seen that dog chasing after you like you were lunch. That thing's big as a Clydesdale."

Elissa clasped her hands to her heart and batted her eyes. "My hero."

That made everyone laugh again, everyone but Pete, anyway. When Ryan Teague walked up and caught the guys' attention, Elissa shook her head and looked back toward Skyler. She'd opened her mouth to speak when something behind Skyler caught her attention and caused her to stop.

"What?"

Skyler turned just as Elissa said, "Don't."

Too late. The sight of Logan Bradshaw leaning against the exterior wall of the inn stole her breath. He made it worse by smiling. Trying to act nonchalant, she slowly broke eye contact and turned back toward Elissa. "What is he doing here?"

"I don't know. You want me to get rid of him?"

"No, it's fine. I don't want to do anything to mess up India's day."

"Pretty sure he's party crashing."

India made her way past a throng of well-wishers to get to Skyler and Elissa. "He didn't," she said. "Liam saw him in the lobby and told him to come out and have a drink."

"But what was he doing in the lobby?" Skyler asked where no one else could hear her. "I was never supposed to see him again."

Elissa squeezed Skyler's hand. "Is that what you really want?"

"I'm finally getting used to the idea of, you know, doing this alone. Finally believing I can do this. I don't need some drifter mucking that up."

India leaned close. "He is the father, hon. Don't you think he deserves to know?"

"Why, because I spent one night with him? I doubt the guy even has a permanent address. A child needs stability, not a dad who floats in and out of his life every time the wind blows."

"You don't know that he'd be like that," India said. "Not until you give him a chance."

Skyler shook her head. "I can't do that. I'm not the first woman he's bedded after a rodeo, and I'd lay my life savings on the fact that I won't be the last."

"But—"

"Oh, crap," Elissa said. "He's heading this way."

Skyler panicked. Why hadn't she made a run for it the moment she saw him? Because that wouldn't have been obvious at all. She'd swear she could feel his heat as he got closer.

"You can do this," Elissa said under her breath.

"I hear congratulations are in order," Logan said as he

stopped so close to Skyler she could reach out and touch him. "You do make a beautiful bride."

India smiled. "Thank you. I think the guys were headed for another drink, if you'd like to join them."

"I'd actually like to ask Skyler to dance. Seems I remember we were pretty good at it last time we twirled around a dance floor."

She glanced at him for a fraction of a second. "Sorry, I'm all out of dance moves for the night."

"Mighty early to be packing it in," he said.

"I've had a long day."

Before she realized what he was doing, he wrapped his hand around hers. "Just one dance."

She glanced at her friends. The look on India's face, that she was on the verge of coming to Skyler's rescue on a day when she should be focusing on nothing other than her new husband, made Skyler's decision for her. "One dance."

Her nerves stretched so thin she feared they'd start popping from the strain, Skyler allowed Logan to guide her into the midst of couples dancing. Keri Teague even gave her a thumbs-up from where she stood next to her sister-in-law Grace.

"You don't seem very happy to see me," Logan said.

"Just surprised. What are you doing here? The next rodeo isn't for another month."

"I do have a cousin here, remember? Plus, I felt the need for a vacation."

She laughed a little at that. "Isn't your entire life a vacation?"

"Whoa, harsh."

"Sorry." She guessed pregnancy came with a side of extra bitchy. "It really has been a long day." And the feel of his big hand pressed to the small of her back wasn't helping. When he tried to tug her closer, she resisted. The irrational fear swelled up in her that if he made contact with her stomach, he'd be able to tell his child was growing inside her.

A small part of her wanted to tell him, to not have to go through this alone, to give him a chance to prove her fears wrong. But she'd had enough upheaval. She needed to do this her way, without someone else, someone who wasn't going to be there all the time, having a say in how she raised her child. She was the responsible one. He was married to the road and adrenaline. She wouldn't have her child constantly looking out the window wondering when Daddy was going to come home.

"Maybe you should turn in early."

She made the mistake of looking up at him in time to see the mischievous look in his eyes. He wasn't suggesting she go to bed alone. She hated how much she had to fight the desire to take him up on his offer, to lift onto the tips of her toes and capture his mouth with hers. Whatever else she might say about him, he drew her physically with a frightening intensity. She had to make everything crystal clear to him once and for all.

"Listen, Logan, you're a nice guy. And we had fun that night. But that's all it was, one night. Our lives are too different. We're nothing alike. So I think the flirting and the innuendo needs to stop because it's not going anywhere." She meant everything she said, and yet every word felt like a bitter lie.

"You trying to convince me or yourself?"

"What?"

"That little speech sounded rehearsed, almost like you've been practicing it since that night I kissed you outside your apartment."

"Why would I do that?"

"I don't know, Miss Harrington." He leaned closer, and before she could pull away, he captured her lips.

She wanted to resist. At least that's what the sane part of her mind was yelling at her. But he tasted so good, and it felt so incredible to be held in his arms again. So she kissed him back, telling herself that this would be the last time. That in a moment she'd be strong again and pull away.

Logan was the one who broke the kiss. It wasn't until the fog in her head cleared and she saw the satisfied smile on his face that common sense overrode pure desire and gave her the strength to extricate herself from him. She searched for words but came up empty. In the end, she simply walked away from him.

She needed to get far from all these people, to have a few minutes to collect her thoughts, to calm down. Hopefully Logan would take the hint and leave. She hurried along the walkway at the front of the inn, increasing her pace as she moved beyond the edge of the crowd. Why had she let herself get wrapped up in that crazy physical attraction again? Logan Bradshaw was dangerous for her peace of mind, for her ability to think with anything resembling even half of her brain.

Skyler scooted to the edge of the walkway to avoid the sprinklers that were trying to keep the landscaping from burning to an absolute crisp.

"Skyler, wait."

She looked over her shoulder at the sound of Logan's voice. Why couldn't he leave her alone? Why did a treasonous part of her not want him to?

She was about to tell him to go back to the party when her foot slipped off the edge of the walkway. Instinctively, she covered her stomach with one hand and reached out to try to break her fall with the other. But the angle was off, and her elbow buckled as soon as her hand hit the ground. She hit hard, knocking the wind out of her.

"Skyler!" Logan ran toward her, reaching her side before she was able to draw a breath. "Are you okay?"

Fear shot through her. "Go get Elissa. Tell her to bring Chloe."

"I can help you."

"Just do it!" She blinked back tears and told herself it wasn't that bad, just a little spill. The baby was fine. Still, she was afraid to move, scared that if she did, it would be a dreadful mistake.

It seemed to take forever for Chloe and Elissa to come around the corner, Logan right next to them. Skyler motioned him away. "Go on back to the party."

"Like hell. I want to make sure you're okay."

"I'm fine."

The way he stared at her, he knew she was lying or at the very least not telling him everything. Why was this happening? She didn't want him to know. Or did she?

"We can help her inside," Elissa said.

Logan still didn't budge, and the tiniest sliver of hope lit inside Skyler, barely discernible amid all the panic but there nonetheless.

"Do you feel like you broke anything?" Chloe said as she knelt beside Skyler. She gave Skyler a meaningful look.

"I don't know. I hit my arm as I fell."

"We should go get an X-ray just to make sure."

Skyler knew what Chloe was doing, giving Skyler a reason to go to the hospital without revealing the real reason they needed to check her out without Logan towering over them.

"Elissa, go on back to the party," Skyler said. "No sense in both of India's bridesmaids pulling a disappearing act."

"You sure?"

"Yeah. I'll go with Chloe, and I'll be back before you know it." She had to believe nothing was wrong, that she hadn't let her need to get away from Logan and her attraction to him endanger her baby. At first she hadn't been sure about even having it, but now she dared anyone or anything to pose even the slightest hint of harm toward her child.

"Can you stand?" Chloe asked.

Before she could answer, Logan was there beside her, wrapping his strong arm around her back and helping her to her feet. Something warm stirred inside Skyler at the look of genuine concern on his face. It was so unlike the normal happy-go-lucky flirt that she wondered how often it made an appearance.

When she was standing, Logan didn't let go, as if he feared she might topple over again.

"Thank you," Chloe said. "I'll take it from here."

"I can drive you to the hospital."

"No need," Skyler said. "Go back and enjoy the party. I hear they have a surprise coming up."

Skyler hated that she was going to miss the heart-shaped fireworks she and Elissa had planned. But she knew she wouldn't be able to calm down until she was certain the baby was okay. It might not look like a baby yet, but that's how she thought of it, as if he or she was already a wee little human. One she was supposed to protect.

As Chloe led her toward the parking lot, Skyler glanced back toward Logan. He still stood on the walkway watching her. She had the oddest sensation that he might feel as alone as he looked. It was almost enough to make her go back and tell him the truth. Almost, but not quite.

"YOU'RE CERTAIN NOTHING'S wrong?" Skyler asked an hour later once Chloe had done a thorough examination and pronounced Skyler and baby perfectly healthy save a small bruise on Skyler's arm.

"Positive. I think the fall scared you more than anything."

"Thank you, for everything." She put a lot of unspoken meaning into those words.

Chloe caught her gaze. "Logan's the father?"

Skyler nodded. "But he doesn't know."

"I figured from the panicked look on your face."

"You won't say anything, will you?"

"I can't. You're my patient. But as your friend, do you mind me asking why you haven't told him?"

"I just don't think it's a good idea." She could have confessed to Chloe and felt secure in it going no further than this examination room, but Skyler suddenly felt too tired to explain. And some little sliver of herself was whispering that her reasons didn't hold water.

But she couldn't depend on her wishy-washy emotions when it came to something this important. Good solid common sense had to be the decider here. And common sense was saying that this child would be better off with one stable parent than the classic two-parent scenario where one parent could never be depended on to be there. A parent needed to be around for not just the big things like birthdays and graduations but also the little ones like scuffed knees, games of tag and Saturday-morning pancakes and cartoons. Hard to be there for those boo-boos when you were off riding some ornery bull in Wyoming or Oklahoma.

"Okay." Chloe didn't say anything other than that one word, but she didn't have to. Her tone said it all.

"You think I'm making a mistake."

Chloe leaned against a supply closet. "Only you can make that decision. All I'll say is I'm not the only one who knows how hard it is to raise a kid alone. People do it all the time, and successfully, but it's not easy." By the sadness in Chloe's eyes, Skyler knew she was thinking about her mother. She'd died in a car wreck when they'd been in elementary school, leaving Chloe's father to raise her and her two brothers alone.

"This is different. I barely know Logan."

"You've got more than seven months to get to know each other before the baby arrives."

"Hard to do if he's not here. His life is on the road."

"Maybe, but he's here now and seemed genuinely concerned about you." Chloe smiled. "And don't think I didn't see that kiss earlier. There's still an attraction there, on both your parts. Who's to say it might not lead to more?"

Skyler rubbed her forehead, trying to stave off a building headache. "I just don't know. All the uncertainty scares me."

"Sorry to tell you this, but life is full of uncertainty. Sometimes it leads to bad things, but sometimes it doesn't. You never know until you open the door and see what's on the other side."

Skyler met her friend's gaze. "I'm not sure you went into the right field. You'd make a good therapist."

Chloe laughed a little. "My brothers would argue I'm just annoying and should mind my own business." She pushed away from the cabinet. "I have faith you'll make the right decision, for you and your baby."

Chloe left the room so Skyler could get dressed. Skyler's fear about telling Logan the truth didn't go away, but she wondered if it was blinding her to what was the right thing to do. Just because Logan was still little more than a stranger didn't mean he didn't deserve to know he was going to be a father. If she told him, nothing had to change. He would most likely still leave, and she'd be a single parent.

Was that fair to her child when Skyler knew how heartbreaking it was to not mean enough for your father to stick around? But could she be so cold as to hide the truth from Logan for his entire life just so she could avoid her fears? And what if something happened to her? Grace Teague had come back to town to tell Nathan he was a father to a little boy because of that same fear, and things had worked out well for them. Not that she thought she and Logan would fall in love and live happily ever after, but he was the only family her child would have if she died.

Pushing the decision away for the moment, she slid off the table and changed out of the hospital gown into her clothes. When she reached the waiting area, she was surprised to see not only Elissa and Chloe but also India and Liam.

"What are you two doing here?"

"Checking on you, silly. We just found out about your fall a few minutes ago."

"I didn't want to ruin your celebration."

"You didn't ruin anything. The party was beginning to break up, anyway."

"Still, the E.R. is not where you should spend your wedding night."

"Don't worry," Liam said. "There's plenty of night left."

India swatted him on the stomach but gave him a look that said she'd make it up to him later. That unwanted pang of longing hit Skyler again.

"Are you okay?" Elissa asked.

"Yeah, everything's fine."

"Thank goodness. You scared the living daylights out of me."

Skyler glanced toward India and Liam.

"I'm sorry, I had to tell him," India said.

Skyler smiled at her, then Liam. "It's okay. He would have found out soon enough, anyway. But I still don't want it to go any further for now. I keep hoping I'll come up with the perfect way to let the cat out of the bag besides a big Ta-da, I'm Preggers. For now all I want to do is go home and curl up in my bed."

"Um, Sky, before we go, you need to know Logan's sitting outside." India nodded toward the exit.

"What?" She looked through the window and, sure enough,

Logan was sitting on the bench in the little courtyard just outside the E.R. entrance. He was nothing if not persistent.

"He was here before any of us," Elissa said. "He was pacing a trench in the floor in here when I got here."

"I know you don't want to tell him about the baby," India said. "But he looked really worried."

Skyler thought she'd have more time to decide for certain what she wanted to do, but that didn't seem to be in Fate's grand plan. Either she told him now and got it over with, or she hid it from him forever. As she stared at him through the window, her heart and her fear duked it out inside her.

"I'll go talk to him." Even if she decided to keep the baby a secret, she could be friendly to him, thank him for his concern. But as she walked outside and saw him turn toward her with that same unexpected fear in his eyes, her heart beat even faster.

Despite the fact that she was tired, achy and not firing on all cylinders, she knew she couldn't hide the truth from him any longer. Even though her fear and anxiety were doing their best to change her mind, some innate sense of right and wrong paired up with Chloe's words to trump them.

"I'm pretty sure this is probably the most boring Saturday night you've ever had," she said.

"No, that would have been the time I got snowed in at a dump of a motel somewhere in the middle-of-nowhere, Montana. The TV only got one little local station, and that went bye-bye at 10 p.m. I think I resorted to counting the stains in the carpet just to have something to do."

"Wow, that does sound like a hot Saturday night."

Quiet settled between them for a few seconds, and she clasped her hands together to keep them from shaking.

"By the lack of a cast, I'm guessing you didn't break anything."

"No, guess I freaked out for no reason. Just a bruise."

"I'm sorry I caused you to fall. I should have just left you alone. I'm not so good with giving up the pursuit, I guess."

Skyler shook her head. "Why are you pursuing me, anyway? There have got to be easier catches, women who don't have personalities like a porcupine."

"You mean other than the fact that you're so gorgeous you could cause a twenty-car pileup?"

Skyler laughed, something she wouldn't have thought possible an hour ago, even moments ago. "You are the king of exaggeration."

"I may lay it on thick sometimes, but right now I'm telling the God's honest truth."

This once, she believed him that he wasn't just feeding her a line. A soft warmth bloomed within her, one that tempted her to believe in him. But just because he was being kind didn't mean he would be good father material. Still, he was her baby's father, and he deserved to know that and to have the opportunity to prove himself one way or the other.

Skyler shifted her gaze to the ground and took a deep breath. "Logan, I… There's a reason I freaked out when I fell earlier." She hesitated, teetering on the edge of no return. "I'm pregnant."

When he didn't say anything, she forced herself to meet his gaze.

"I'm sorry, I didn't know you were with someone else. I don't make a habit of hitting on other guys' girls."

His response surprised her and made her a little angry. But she tamped the anger down. After all, he didn't know her any better than she knew him. She swallowed against the dryness in her throat.

"I haven't been with anyone recently but you. The baby's yours."

Logan's forehead scrunched up. "That's impossible. We used protection. That's one thing I'm not careless about."

"Obviously, it failed."

Logan stood and took a couple of steps away. He took a deep breath before he turned back toward her. "What about you? Weren't you on the Pill?"

"No."

"Why the hell not?"

She jerked at his question, and then she released the hold she had on her anger. It wasn't as if she'd planned this to trap him. "Medical reasons."

"God, I can't believe this."

"You know, it wasn't exactly in my life plan either. Not like this, anyway."

He glanced toward the hospital, where her friends were no doubt watching every move she and Logan made. "You weren't going to tell me, were you?"

"No, I wasn't."

"Why not?"

"Because you're not the staying-in-one-place type. But don't worry, I don't expect you to." She tried not to remember Chloe's reminder of how hard it would be to raise a child on her own.

"You don't know me anywhere near as well as you think you do."

"I know you well enough, Logan." She stopped, took a slow breath to calm herself. Nothing good would come from them arguing out here where anyone could hear and see them. Besides, how had she expected him to act? She hadn't exactly reacted with smiles and hurrahs when she'd found out. "My father was a lot like you. Maybe you have the best of intentions of doing the right thing, but the call of something new and exciting will always take you away. And I can tell you from experience that's a pretty rotten way to grow up, never knowing when and if you'll ever see your father again." She took a deep breath. "I don't think you're a bad person, but your idea of how to live life is different than mine. Just because I told you about the baby doesn't mean I expect anything from you."

"That makes me sound lousy."

"That's not what I meant. This just isn't your responsibility. You didn't ask for it."

"Neither did you."

"No, but I've accepted it. I can love this child enough for two parents. I know how because I watched my mother do it every day until she died."

"That's not fair to you."

"I'm not really a believer in life being fair. It's only what we make it. And I intend to make life as happy and safe for this child as I possibly can."

And hopefully neither she nor her child would ache with loneliness and for something that could never be.

Chapter Ten

Logan had no doubt Skyler would do everything she said, but anger simmered in him that she'd made all these decisions without him as if his opinion didn't matter. Even though she'd changed her mind about telling him about the baby, he might have gone through the rest of his life never knowing about his son or daughter.

"It's not just your child, Skyler."

"Not biologically, no. But a child's future should be shaped by the parent who is there on a daily basis. Are you willing to commit to that, Logan? Staying in one place, changing diapers, helping with homework, going to parent-teacher conferences, listening when her heart is broken by the first boy who loves her?"

He wanted to say yes, even opened his mouth to do so, but nothing came out. Instead, it felt as if chains started wrapping themselves around his legs, tying him down, trapping him in a world not of his choosing.

The look of disappointment on Skyler's face punched him in the gut, but he still didn't speak.

"I'm not angry, Logan. I'm simply making the best of an unexpected situation." She took a deep breath. "I just thought you should know." She hesitated a moment longer, as if waiting for him to say something, before she glanced toward the hospital, then headed toward the parking lot.

No matter how hard he tried, he couldn't find the words to stop her. Probably there weren't any, because she was right. The idea of settling down and being a dad freaked him out. He wasn't cut out to be a parent. Maybe Skyler had been right to keep him in the dark. If he couldn't be there for her and the child all the time, did he even have the right to call himself the kid's father?

And what did he know about being a father, anyway? The only example he'd had was a man who had no desire to see any part of the world outside of his little sphere, a man who was satisfied to get by, to exist day to day in a life that would drive Logan mad. On the opposite end of the spectrum, he couldn't imagine Skyler allowing him to expose the child to half of the things he'd done. There was probably a middle ground between his and his father's life experiences, but he had no idea how to find it.

When Skyler's friends followed in her wake, he caught Elissa's gaze. The look in her eyes was one part curiosity, one part warning. India, on the other hand, appeared sympathetic, as if she understood the turmoil he was feeling. Liam didn't make eye contact, no doubt as uncomfortable as Logan was.

After they all left, Logan sank onto the bench outside the E.R. and sat there for probably half an hour with his thoughts racing.

Finally, he eyed his own truck. Feeling as if he'd been hit half a dozen times with a stun gun, he shook his head and walked toward the parking area. Instead of calling Jesse again, he just drove out to his cousin's house. The light was on in the front room, so he parked beside Jesse's truck, grabbed his bag and headed for the side door. But when he banged on the door, he got no response.

"Hey, Jess, it's Logan."

He was beginning to think Jesse was dead asleep when the door that led into his cousin's kitchen opened. Jesse stood there with no shirt and his belt unbuckled and hanging loose from his belt loops.

"Dude, so not a good time."

Logan's head was trapped in such a fog that it took him a moment to pick up on what was going on. "Sorry, man. Didn't know you were occupied."

"Call next time."

"I did. You didn't answer."

"Again, busy."

Suddenly bone weary, Logan asked, "When do you think you'll be done being busy? I'd like to bum your couch for a few days." While he figured out how to deal with the news that he was going to be a dad.

Jesse didn't answer at first and shifted uncomfortably on his bare feet. "Sorry, but I'm not living alone anymore."

"Oh."

Jesse cocked his head slightly to the side and leaned his forearm against the doorframe. "You all right?"

Logan managed to nod. For now he wasn't sharing his news with anyone. Besides, his cousin looked like a man who very much wanted to get back to what he'd been doing. "Yeah. Sorry to bother you." Before Jesse could question why Logan wasn't teasing him unmercifully, Logan started back toward his truck.

But when he slid into the driver's seat, he had no idea where to go. Should he go to Skyler's apartment and talk to her some more? Or should he stay away until he could think straight? It didn't help his state of mind or his mood when the lower part of his back started aching where he'd wrenched it during that last bull ride.

As he drove back toward Blue Falls, he thought of those pillow-soft beds at the Wildflower Inn. Part of him liked the idea of staying under Skyler's roof and gradually figuring out how they would deal with being parents. Instead, he decided to go with the more economical option, the one that would give him time to rest before he had to face Skyler and the truth again, and headed for the Country Vista. After all, it wasn't without its pleasant memories, even if that night had led to the scariest thing he'd ever faced.

By the time he registered and got his key, his back was hurting even more. He needed a hot shower, a couple of ibuprofen and a good night's rest. It didn't hit him until he was standing outside his room that it was the same one he'd stayed in before. Despite everything, he laughed a little. He had to say he would much rather be escorting Skyler through the doorway than his aching body and the realization that his life was never going to be the same again.

DESPITE THE LONG, stressful day before, Skyler woke the next morning just as daylight was creeping into her apartment. She lay in the bed staring at the ceiling, her thoughts picking up where they'd left off when she'd finally fallen asleep sometime after midnight. She'd started second-guessing her decision to tell Logan about the baby the moment the words had left her mouth, but deep down she knew she'd done the right thing. And whatever came of that revelation, she'd find a way to deal with it, just as she had every other challenge life had thrown at her.

By the time she was up and dressed, the sun was peeking over the horizon and she was determined to have a good day and not worry herself into a tizzy. She headed for the inn's dining room just as she normally did each morning.

"You're up early," said Amber, one of the morning-shift waitresses.

"Yes, it must be a sign of the end times or something, me being up before the sun."

Amber laughed. "Can I get you anything?"

"No, thanks."

As Amber headed toward one of the tables next to the window, where an early-rising couple sat, Skyler walked toward the beverage station. The aroma of the coffee drew her, and she took a moment to inhale the wonderful smell. Oh, how she missed coffee. With a sigh, she grabbed a glass and filled it with milk.

"Now *that* is a sign of the end times," Amber said as she grabbed a couple of cups and began to pour coffee.

Skyler almost moaned at the delicious scent. "I've been drinking way too much caffeine. I'm turning over a new leaf." She'd been abstaining for a while now, but she'd managed to hide that fact.

"Yeah, good luck with that." Amber sounded as if she thought that might last about half a day.

If Skyler weren't carrying a child, Amber would probably be right.

She took her glass of milk and a plain bagel outside and sat on one of the benches overlooking the park at the bottom of the hill. People had already begun returning since the work on the dock and picnic shelters had been completed, but she really wanted some of the moneymaking projects under way before the baby came. Her time would be at even more of a premium with an infant to care for, and she could use the extra monetary cushion concessions would bring in. She didn't want her child to ever worry about if the bills were going to get paid or see his mother working herself to death just to make ends meet. Her child would have as happy and carefree a childhood as she could make it.

Maybe Logan would help shoulder the responsibilities.

No, she couldn't depend on that. Especially not judging by his silence as she'd walked away the night before.

"Hey, hon. Are you feeling okay?"

Skyler looked over to see India walking toward her. "What

are you doing up? I would think you'd be sleeping in with that new husband of yours."

"Don't worry, I had plenty of time in bed last night." India grinned at the memory, causing Skyler to smile. "I just wanted to get in a nice walk this morning before we head to the airport. Going to be cooped up in planes for the rest of the day."

"Yes, but tonight you'll be lying on the beach in Hawaii while the rest of us are baking our brains out here."

"True." India sat beside her. "You didn't answer my question. Are you okay this morning?"

"Yes, fine."

"Have you heard from Logan?"

"No, but that's okay. I did what was right, telling him. Now I'll just move ahead as I planned all along." And try to forget the daydream she'd briefly allowed herself of the two of them making a life for their child together. When she really thought about it, that daydream didn't even make sense. Logan was barely an acquaintance.

"I don't feel right leaving you here like this."

Skyler playfully swatted India's hand. "Don't be silly. You deserve this trip and your happiness more than anyone I know. So don't you dare give me another thought. I want to see tons of pictures of waves, beaches, luaus and I wouldn't mind a hot surfer or two." Despite her words, it wasn't a buff surfer that popped into her mind. It was a certain cowboy she couldn't get out of her head.

India squeezed Skyler's hand. "You gave us quite a scare last night."

"Sorry. I overreacted."

"Better safe than sorry." India looked toward the lake when a duck quacked as it floated along the surface with a few of its friends. "I can't remember the last time I saw you up this early. But I guess it's good practice."

"Ugh, don't remind me. I'll probably win the World's Grumpiest Mother award."

India smiled. "You're going to be wonderful."

"I'm not so sure about that."

"I am."

Skyler looked at her friend. "What makes you say that?"

"Because you're a hard worker, strong, determined and most of all, full of love. You've always been a wonderful friend to me, even when I didn't have many. And that's going to translate to being a fantastic mother."

"I hope you're right. I keep thinking about all the ways I can mess this up."

"You worry too much. And you don't know what the future holds. You might not have to do this alone."

"I'm not holding my breath."

Silence settled between them for several moments.

"So I guess your plans for the park are on indefinite hold," India said, as if sensing Skyler wanted to change the topic of conversation.

"Actually, I was thinking about that before you came up. I would like to have at least part, if not all, of it up and running before the baby gets here. I'm just worried about sinking so much money into it."

"I think it's a good investment, especially since the rodeos seem to be bringing even more people to town. I heard from Verona that one of the Dallas TV stations is going to do a travel piece on Blue Falls. Maybe if you at least had things started, they could include the park offerings when they talk about the inn."

Skyler stared at the park, imagining all her plans coming to life, the area full of locals and tourists having a good time. Just the day before, in the midst of showing the musicians where to set up for the wedding, she'd gotten the idea for concerts in the park.

"If I could just sell the ranch, I wouldn't worry so much about sinking money into something new. And it's not just me I have to consider anymore."

"When was the last time you had anyone look at the ranch?"

Skyler shrugged. "Maybe six months ago. I kept hoping it would sell as is, but I may have to cave and hire someone to do some work on the place, make it more attractive to buyers. Maybe I can talk to Len. He and his son did a good job on the shelters and the dock."

"I don't know if he'll have time. I heard a couple of days ago that he just got a job with a builder in Kerrville."

Skyler sighed.

"Have Elissa ask around. She works with lots of landscapers, so they're bound to know some handyman types looking for work."

That wasn't a bad idea. And if she could somehow get it taken care of without having to be too hands-on, so much the better.

"Well, I better get in and take a shower," India said.

"Have a nice fruity drink on the beach for me while you're there, okay?"

"You got it. And you take care of yourself. If you need help, ask Elissa or Verona, Keri, one of your employees. They don't have to know why you're asking."

"I will, I promise."

India patted her hand, then headed inside. When Skyler was alone again, she watched the ducks gliding across the water and smiled. The thought of getting the ranch in better shape, of maybe finally being able to sell it, gave her a boost of excitement. Now that the idea was planted, she couldn't wait to put it into motion.

IT TOOK ANOTHER couple of ibuprofen to get going the next morning, but once Logan was up and moving, he could tell his back was a little better than it had been the day before. At least that's what he told himself. He wasn't one to admit to pain or even sickness unless it absolutely knocked him on his ass. Besides, there were bigger things to think about than a backache.

Before he could make any decisions about his day, he had to eat. He'd not eaten anything since he'd been halfway between Houston and Blue Falls the day before, and his stomach felt like an empty pit. As soon as he was dressed, he headed straight for the Primrose Café. The place was packed as usual when he walked in. As he eyed the room, someone waving caught his attention. It was Verona, who was sitting with Elissa.

He resisted the urge to turn around and leave. Instead, he approached their table. "Good morning, ladies."

Verona patted the empty chair next to her. "Have a seat. You look like a man in need of breakfast."

He caught a warning on Elissa's face as he sat, then a subtle shake of her head as she glanced at Verona. When it hit him that Verona must not know about Skyler's pregnancy, he gave Elissa a quick nod back. Still, he'd been seen at the hospital last night, so he figured simply mentioning Skyler wasn't off-limits.

"How's Skyler this morning?"

"Fine." Elissa didn't elaborate.

"We were just talking about her," Verona said, evidently oblivious to the odd reaction from her niece. "Do you or your cousin happen to know any good handymen in the area?"

"Jesse might. I really don't know many people here. Is she needing more work done at that park?"

"Eventually, but now she's looking for someone to fix up her family's old ranch so she can sell it."

"What all needs to be done?"

"Don't worry about it," Elissa said. "We'll find someone."

"Some upkeep-type repairs to the house, cleaning out vegetation, fixing some broken fencing. That kind of stuff."

"Verona, don't bother him with this. He already said he doesn't know anyone."

A crazy idea burst to life in Logan's head, a way for him to spend more time in Blue Falls getting to know Skyler. After all, she was the mother of his child. A voice in his mind whispered that wasn't the only reason he wanted to spend time with her. There was something about Skyler that made it difficult for him not to think about her.

"I might be able to do it. I had lots of practice growing up on a ranch."

"Oh, that's perfect," Verona said, smiling and looking as if she wanted to clap.

"Won't you be leaving soon, on to the next rodeo?" Elissa asked.

What a difference a few weeks and news of a pregnancy made. Before, she was all about getting him and Skyler together. Now she seemed to want to boot him out of town. Was that what Skyler wanted, too? Had he royally screwed up his response to her news the night before?

Well, he wasn't going anywhere. Not yet, anyway. He might not be a put-down-roots type of guy, but he wasn't one to abandon his child either. Honestly, he didn't know how he was going to handle things, but he wasn't going to be run out of town before he figured it out.

"I'm taking a couple of weeks off." Surely by then he and Skyler could come to some sort of understanding. And maybe the time away from riding would give his back a chance to fully heal.

"Great timing," Verona said. "When you get finished with breakfast, you head on down to the real estate office. Tell Justine I sent you and to give you the listing for the ranch. That will give you directions on how to get there."

As he finished placing his order, he noticed Elissa tossing money down on the table and making moves to leave.

"Where you going, honey?" Verona asked. "You've barely touched your breakfast."

"Not all that hungry this morning. And I have a ton of work to do at the nursery."

After Elissa nearly raced for the door, Verona shook her head. "That's got to be the first time I've ever seen that girl leave breakfast behind when she wasn't sick."

Logan would lay a substantial wad of cash on a bet that she was heading straight to the Wildflower Inn to tell Skyler all about his interest in working at the ranch for a few days.

"I know that look," Verona said.

He shifted his attention to the older woman. "Is that right?"

"That's the look of a man who knows what he wants and intends to go after it."

He picked up his coffee cup and took a drink. Chances were Verona had a better idea of what he wanted than he did.

"She what?" Skyler asked a lot more loudly than she'd intended. When she realized she'd drawn the attention of a couple of her employees as well as three women who were checking into the inn, she grabbed Elissa's arm and pulled her down the hallway to her office, then shut the door behind them. "Tell me you're teasing me for some cruel reason."

Elissa shook her head. "I'm afraid not. I couldn't stop her without being obvious and drawing questions I didn't think you wanted asked. To his credit, Logan didn't spill the beans."

Skyler paced the narrow width of the office. "Maybe I'll just tell him I've changed my mind, that I can't afford the repairs right now."

"Don't you think he'll see that for what it is, you avoiding him? I thought you were okay with having told him about the baby."

"I am. It's just…if he's going to eventually leave, I'd rather he do it now."

"You're afraid of getting used to him being here and then the rug being pulled out from under you."

Skyler looked out the window. "Yeah."

"Is it more than that?"

Skyler sighed and probably took too long to answer. "No."

Chances were Elissa could tell Skyler was still attracted to Logan and didn't quite trust herself where he was concerned, but she didn't point that out.

Skyler glanced at Elissa. "What do you think I should do?"

"I can't tell you that."

Skyler raised an eyebrow. "Since when do you pass up an opportunity to tell me how to live my life?"

"Since it really matters. All I'll say is don't let your decision come out of fear. But whatever you decide, I've got your back."

"Thanks."

Long after Elissa left, Skyler sat staring out the window, her thoughts bouncing back and forth like a ball in a tennis match. If she told Logan she wasn't ready to work on the ranch, maybe he'd leave town sooner and stay away this time. But was that what she really wanted? Could something good possibly come of Logan staying for a while only to leave later? Should she get to know him better so she'd have stories to tell their child? Should she allow him to work at the ranch in hopes that the eventual sale would help ensure the baby's future? She wished for a crystal ball that would show her how different decisions would play out.

Her head began to throb with all the trains of thought colliding in her mind. She leaned back in her chair and closed her eyes. It didn't take long before she felt herself drifting toward sleep. A knock on her door jerked her fully awake.

"Sorry. I didn't mean to scare you. I seem to have a habit of that, don't I?"

"Yes, you do. Maybe that can be your second career. 'Need to scare the living daylights out of someone? Call Logan Bradshaw for all your scaring needs.'"

Logan smiled, and it caused her heart to toss in a few extra beats. Why did the man have to be so damn attractive?

He leaned his shoulder against the doorframe. "I talked to Verona and Elissa this morning about you looking for someone to do some repairs out on your ranch."

"I heard."

"And you've already decided to tell me no."

"I didn't say that. It's just...it's a big undertaking, and it won't be cheap. I've let the place go."

"You wouldn't have to pay me."

"What?" Of all the ways this conversation could have gone, his offer of working for free hadn't been one she'd imagined.

"Seems I can't stay at my cousin's place, because he has a new roommate, so I thought I could do the repairs in exchange for staying in the house out there."

She stared at him, trying to figure out what was really going on in his head. "Why would you want to do that? The house probably smells like it's been closed up for years." Because it had been.

Logan took a couple more steps into the room. "I don't want to crowd you, but I want to get to know you better."

Skyler's skin warmed at the look in his eyes, as if he might be standing there saying the same thing even if there were no baby. She mentally shook her head, telling herself she couldn't get too attached. Logan was a good-time type of guy, not the settle-down-and-raise-babies kind. She couldn't even fault him for that, because he'd never claimed to be anything other than he was.

But what about what he'd said the night before?

You don't know me anywhere near as well as you think you do.

That was just one of those things people said when some-one was making assumptions about them, right?

"Handyman work would be a little tame for your tastes, wouldn't it?"

He smiled that mischievous smile that had drawn her to his bed. "Even skydiving cowboys have to take a break now and then."

Not trusting her willpower, she frantically searched for a reason to decline his offer but came up empty. Maybe this, like telling him the truth about the baby, was a leap of faith she needed to take.

"Come on, how can you pass up free labor? And I dare you to find a handyman who's more charming than I am."

She shook her head. "Does your mama know what a piece of work she raised?"

His smile dimmed, enough that she wished she could take back her words. Just when she thought she had him totally pegged, he showed her some emotion that she didn't expect. First his concern when she'd fallen the night before, then the fact that he hadn't run as soon as he'd heard the word *baby*. Now here was a hint that there was something not so great regarding his mother. Had he lost her? She swallowed past a sudden lump in her throat. Would her baby have no grand-parents at all?

Logan had said he wanted to get to know her better, and now she found herself feeling the same way about him. But could she do that and still guard her emotions for when he inevitably left?

"Fine, you can stay at the house. Let me go get the key."

When she came out of the apartment with the key, he was waiting for her in the hallway.

"Remember the last time we stood out here?"

Her entire body flushed with the memory. That kiss, she could still feel it as if it had happened only moments ago. Instead of answering him, she extended the key.

He gave her a knowing smile, then took the key, deliberately brushing her fingers with his. "So what all would you like done?"

"Whatever you can do to spruce up the curb appeal. It's been on the market for quite a while, and I'd like to be rid of it."

"Property taxes killing you?"

"Yeah." And the memories every time she went out there.

Logan tossed the key up in the air a little, then caught it. "Well, I better get to work." He tapped the edge of his hat, gave her a little bow. "Ma'am." And then he turned and walked down the hall.

She had to admit she liked the old, flirty Logan better than the freaked-out version she'd seen the night before. It made her remember their one night together. Despite everything, it had been one of the best nights of her life. Even if Logan disappeared, she doubted her memories of that night or how she'd felt in his arms ever would.

She caught herself watching how very nicely those jeans encased his legs and butt as he walked away. And then remembering what those legs had felt like sliding along hers. Thank goodness he didn't turn around and catch her ogling.

She swallowed against the dryness in her throat and walked slowly back into her office. She sank into her chair and thought about Logan walking across the land where she'd played as a child. He would eat in the kitchen where her mother had made her breakfast and dinner every day no matter how tired she was. He would mend the fences she'd helped her father mend whenever he was home. And he might even sleep in her bed, staring up at the ceiling she'd looked at while she imagined what life would be like if her father would just come home and stay.

But all too soon, she feared, Logan would walk out the front door and drive away just as her father had time and time again. Only Skyler was determined she would not mourn as her mother had.

No matter how many times she told herself that, it never felt like the truth.

Chapter Eleven

Logan sank onto the porch swing, a cold beer in hand, wiped out from everything he'd done that day. He'd been at work on the ranch for a week, and he was surprised how much he'd actually enjoyed it. He was normally a social guy, always up for a party, but something about the solitude for the past few days had seemed to be exactly what he needed.

As he worked, he'd run countless scenarios in his head of how the next few months of his life might unfold. He wondered if he could stay in Blue Falls until Skyler had the baby, maybe find work to help offer support while he wasn't riding. But would he be able to go for good after seeing the baby, leaving Skyler during the difficult first months with a newborn?

He made decent money riding the circuit. Maybe he could stick with it but not ride as often, requiring less travel. Or would he be helping more by riding and offering Skyler monetary support? He feared she might be right about him and his inability to settle down. Though he'd enjoyed his time here on the ranch, was he willing to commit to this type of life long term, or would he start going stir-crazy?

He ran his hand over his face, pushing thoughts of the distant future away. Best to take things as they came, dealing with only what was right in front of him. For now at least, he was staying and helping as he should.

That's not the only reason you're staying.

No, it wasn't. He'd found himself daydreaming about Skyler the woman just as often, more even, than Skyler the mother of his child.

He'd imagined a dozen different places around the ranch where he could steal kisses or make love to her, including the bed where he'd been sleeping. He knew it had been hers as a girl because of the light purple paint on the walls and a couple of teen-idol posters she'd left behind.

It was hard to imagine her as a little girl on this ranch, even more difficult to imagine her fitting in here now. She was always so well put together with perfect clothes, not a hair out of place. Well, he'd seen her once when her hair was wild and crazy, and he wouldn't mind seeing it that way again. If she came out to the ranch and they managed to make it to her bed, she could scream her pleasure and no one would hear but him.

Logan squirmed as his body reacted to his memories of Skyler beneath him. What was it about this one woman that tugged at him so much? He'd given her several days to get used to him being in town, hoping she'd come out to the ranch. And not just to talk about the baby. He wanted to see her beautiful face, hear her voice, maybe even kiss those delectable lips again. Could he convince her that they were good together and that she shouldn't fight their mutual attraction so hard? Only one way to find out.

He cleaned up, changed and headed into town. Not wanting to show up empty-handed, he stopped by a florist on the way and picked out a bouquet of pink and purple flowers. He couldn't name a single one of them, but that didn't matter. If they melted her resistance to him even a little, they would have done their job.

He stopped by Gino's Pizza to pick up the second phase of his hastily put-together plan, made one more stop, then headed toward one of the new picnic shelters at the park.

When he got everything set out on the table, he called Skyler. He'd begun to think his plan had been for naught when she finally answered.

"Hello?"

"Hey, it's Logan."

"Oh, hi. Is something wrong?"

"No, but I'd like to talk to you about the ranch repairs. Can you meet me down at the park?"

"We can just discuss it on the phone."

"But I'm at the park now with a pizza that's way too big for me to eat by myself."

In the silence that followed, he thought he heard her sigh.

"Logan, I don't think—"

"It's a pizza, Skyler. You've got to eat sometime."

Another sigh. "Fine. I'll be there in a few minutes."

"Pizza's better when it's hot."

She hung up, and he had to smile when she walked out the front door of the inn less than a minute later. He watched her during her entire walk down the hill. Damn, the woman was beautiful, like a flame-haired goddess. If he were a smarter man, he'd know he wasn't worthy of her. He wondered if their baby would be a redhead like Skyler. If it was a girl, he'd have to stick around to beat the boys off with a very large stick.

When she reached the picnic shelter, she eyed the table. "I thought you said it was just pizza."

"Oh, did I forget to mention flowers and chocolate cupcakes? Silly me."

With a gentle shake of her head, she took a seat on the bench opposite him. "Well, I'd hate for food to go to waste."

He smiled, glad she seemed to have relaxed somewhat and was willing to spend time with him. "I knew you were a practical woman."

She pulled a slice of pizza from the box. "So, how are the repairs coming?"

"Good. You should come out and take a look."

"No, thanks. I trust you."

"Well, that doesn't seem wise. I could have painted the house pink with giant green polka dots."

She smiled, and it gave him a funny buzzy feeling in his chest.

"I think I would have heard about that," she said before taking a bite of her pizza.

After a short lull, he asked, "How are you feeling?"

"Okay, more tired than I like. But at least the nausea has eased."

"Is there anything I can do to help?"

Skyler met his gaze and for a moment looked as if she were trying to figure out the mysteries of the universe. Finally, she appeared to come to some sort of conclusion. "You're already doing it, helping with the ranch. Getting rid of it will be a big help."

When you're gone and I'm alone.

She didn't say the words, but he heard them all the same. The overwhelming urge to prove her wrong, to tell her that he wasn't going to bail on her welled up in his chest, surprising him.

As they sat and talked about their day, Logan realized he couldn't remember the last time he'd just sat and talked to a woman like this without every word he said working toward getting her into bed. Would he love to sleep with Skyler again? Hell, yes. But just talking about the mundane aspects of day-to-day life gave him an odd sense of happiness.

"I'm surprised you haven't gotten bored out of your mind out there yet," she said.

"Honestly, I'm surprised, too. I grew up on a ranch, in North Dakota, and I couldn't wait to leave. It was so deadly dull that I thought I might go bonkers before I graduated high school."

When Skyler didn't say anything, he realized he'd just given her more evidence to fuel her belief that he would be gone the next time the wind changed directions. Maybe the best thing was to be honest, admit that he probably would go back to the circuit at some point. But he also had to make her believe he wasn't going to totally disappear.

"But I've liked staying out at your ranch," he continued. "It's a nice break from the road."

"Do you ever think you'll stop traveling all the time?"

"Honestly, I don't know. I think I have a few good riding years left. Bull riding is one of those things you've got to do when you're young, when you can still bounce back from injuries."

"Don't you feel like you're just rolling the dice every time you ride? I mean, it's literally life-and-death."

"Once you start, it's hard to give it up. It's like nothing else in the world. Man versus beast."

"I guess I find real life exciting enough."

"That is my real life. At least part of it. That doesn't mean I'm not going to do right by you and the baby."

The expression on Skyler's face tugged at his heart. She looked as though she wanted to believe him but was afraid to.

"Don't make any promises. Then you won't break them."

Part of him wanted to be angry. But he didn't let it show. No matter what he said, she wasn't going to fully believe it until he proved it with actions.

Skyler stayed a few more minutes, making small talk, but he could tell she wanted to leave.

"I need to get back to work," she said.

"You haven't had your dessert yet."

She eyed the cupcake. He thought for a moment she would refuse to take it, but then she grabbed the one nearest her. "I'll eat it later."

He picked up the bouquet and extended it to her. "Don't forget your flowers."

She accepted them. "Thank you. Purple is my favorite color." She sounded touched, as if it had been a long time since someone had given her flowers or done something as simple as guess her favorite color. He didn't know whether that made him sad or angry. As he watched her walk away with the flowers held up to her nose, he thought maybe it was both.

SKYLER LEANED BACK from her computer and rubbed her neck. A morning of doing payroll and accounting had her wishing she could go for a massage. Her gaze drifted over to the bouquet of mixed flowers at the edge of her desk. She touched one of the soft petals and smiled. Gestures like the bouquet, the cupcakes and the pizza picnic were threatening to make her believe that Logan was a different sort of man than he was. But by his own admission, he loved the road and the excitement bull riding provided. And the way he'd talked about his early years on a ranch was yet another reason why she had to guard her heart against wishing for something that couldn't be.

The sound of a siren drew her attention to the window. A fire engine raced up the road past the inn. The local fire fighters had been kept busy ever since the dry spell had become a full-fledged drought. Brush fires popped up all over the county, caused by everything from lightning to idiots who threw their cigarettes out their windows as they drove down the road.

Her phone rang, drawing her attention away from the window.

"Skyler Harrington."

"Skyler, it's Pete. The fire department has been called out to your ranch."

Her chest felt tight as she thought of Logan out there by himself. "What happened?"

"Brush fire, but it's close to the house."

"Okay." She hung up the phone and grabbed her purse. She raced to her car and drove the road she'd driven more times than she could count.

She saw the smoke a couple of miles before she reached the ranch. As she turned into the driveway, she spotted the firemen hosing down a line of flames a few yards from the house. Even though the danger was nearly past, her heart hammered against her ribs. As she hurried from the car, she searched for Logan and found him sitting at the back of the ambulance with an oxygen mask over his nose and mouth.

"Oh, my God," she said as she crossed to him. "Are you okay?"

His eyes widened when he saw her. When he pulled the mask away, the paramedic gave him an exasperated look.

"I'm fine," Logan said. He fixed his gaze on Skyler. When he glanced at her stomach with concern, her heart swelled. Here he was hooked up to oxygen and his thoughts were for their child. When his eyes met hers again, she couldn't help wanting to believe that his concern was for her, as well.

"He inhaled a good bit of smoke," the paramedic said.

Even though Logan sat right in front of Skyler, fear leaped inside her. "What happened?"

He shook his head. "Not sure. I came back from town and it was already racing toward the house. Called 911, then beat it back the best I could. I'm afraid the little shed at the edge of the yard is toast."

"Don't worry about the shed. It was probably nothing more than a home for critters, anyway." How could he think that a shed would matter when he could have been seriously injured or worse? A lump formed in her throat.

"Wasn't for you, the house would have been a goner," said Andrew Canton, one of the firemen.

Skyler kept her gaze on Logan as he watched the firemen put out the last of the blaze and start rolling up the hose on the pumper truck. Logan was drenched in sweat and covered in soot and dirt. She fought the urge to pull him into her arms and kiss him, both for what he'd done and the fact that he was safe.

"Is he okay?" she asked the paramedic, a middle-aged woman she didn't know. "Does he need to go to the hospital?"

Logan shifted his gaze to Skyler and smiled, his teeth bright against the black soot coating his face. "Be careful. You're going to make me think you care."

"He's fine," the paramedic said. "Stubborn, but fine."

Logan stepped away from the ambulance to allow the paramedic to stow her gear.

"What were you thinking?" Skyler asked.

"That I was saving your house."

"No house is worth you getting killed."

"No, but I didn't get killed. You heard the lady. I'm fine." Then why was she shaking?

"Though I'm not so sure about you," Logan said, turning serious again. "You look like you need to sit down." He wrapped his arm around her shoulders and guided her to the edge of the porch. He didn't let go until she was sitting with her feet dangling over what had once been her mother's flowerbeds.

"You don't need to get upset like this," he said, his voice so gentle she almost leaned into him.

"Then don't scare me." Skyler looked up and met Logan's eyes. "I'm glad you're okay."

"And you thought I'd be bored out here."

She laughed a little, suddenly thankful for the way he had

of easing her anxiety with humor. "This wasn't exactly what I had in mind for entertainment."

He gave her a crooked grin. "What did you have in mind?"

She shook her head. "I swear, you would flirt if they were rolling you into surgery."

"If the nurses were cute."

Brett Markham, the fire chief, walked up to them then. "It's all out and we gave the entire area an extra good dousing. Looks like it started out by the road. Could have been a cigarette or a spark from a passing vehicle. I'll be damn glad when the drought is finally over."

"That makes two of us," Logan said as he extended his hand. The two men shook.

"Skyler, you're lucky you had someone working out here."

"She is, isn't she?" Logan teased. "That's got to be worth dinner, don't you think?"

Brett held up his hands. "Sorry, man. You're on your own there."

As the emergency crews loaded up and headed back toward town, Skyler noticed a line of dried blood on Logan's hand. Before she could think better of it, she grasped his hand and pulled it up where she could see his injury better. The blood originated at a cut across his knuckle.

"We should clean this," she said as she slid off the porch to her feet.

"I'm okay."

"Don't argue." She tugged him toward the steps.

"Yes, ma'am."

Skyler wondered about her sanity the moment she stepped across the threshold. She'd not been inside the house in more than a year, and then only long enough to do a quick check to make sure no windows were broken and no animals had gotten inside. Memories assaulted her but she pushed past them toward the kitchen. She led Logan to the sink and turned on the water. Not trusting him to do a thorough job of cleaning it, she guided his hand below the stream of water and grabbed the bar of plain soap he must have bought. She forced herself not to meet his gaze as she cleaned away the dried blood and then the layers of dirt and smoke.

"You know, I can do this myself," Logan said.

"Oh, no. I'm not having you do a half-baked job, letting it get infected and your hand fall off."

Logan chuckled. "A little exaggerated, don't you think?"

She stopped cleaning his hand but didn't let it go. "I can't believe you tried to fight that fire by yourself."

"I wasn't going to stand by while it burned your house to the ground."

"It's not my house, not anymore."

Logan was uncharacteristically quiet for long enough that she looked up at him.

"Maybe you don't live here anymore, and maybe you have good reasons. But it's still yours, and you need it to bring a better price when you sell the ranch."

That was true, but she didn't want it at the cost of some-one's life. Her heart squeezed at the thought of what might have happened.

He lifted his hand and rubbed his thumb across her cheek. She thought he might kiss her, and in that moment she wanted him to. Instead, he retrieved his hand and wet a paper towel. He brought it to her cheek.

"Sorry, I smudged you."

After he finished, he stared down at her for what felt like a very long time. The fact that it was only moments told her she was treading in dangerous territory if she wanted to maintain the necessary distance between them. She took a step away from him. "I should get back to the inn."

He grasped her hand. "Don't go. Not yet."

"Logan."

"If you won't let me take you out, at least stay for a little while. I don't have anything fancy here, but I can slap together a mean ham-and-turkey sandwich." He smiled. "It's the least you can do for your one-man fire-fighting crew."

"Resorting to guilt trips now?"

"Is it working?"

She took a deep breath and looked out the kitchen window before shifting her gaze back to him. "Okay, but this doesn't mean anything more than two acquaintances hanging out for a bit."

"Whatever you say, sweetheart."

She could never acknowledge how much hearing him call her sweetheart caused her insides to flutter, especially when she thought about how many women he'd probably showered with the same endearment.

"Let me take a quick shower so I'm not so disgusting."

The thought of him getting naked caused heat to radiate throughout her body. When she heard him turn on the shower, she moved away from the sound by walking down the hallway to her old bedroom. She crossed the room to where he'd obviously been sleeping in her bed. With no one to see what she was doing, she stretched out on the mattress. He must have washed the linens, because they smelled like a combination of laundry detergent and his male scent.

She stared out the window at the wide blue sky and remembered lying here as a girl, looking up at that sky and wondering where under its wide expanse her father was at that moment. She closed her eyes as more memories began playing like a film in her head. She knew she was drifting, even heard the shower shut off in the distance, but she couldn't seem to make herself move. Despite the fact that she'd left this house and this room as soon as she could, there was something that felt strangely right about being back here. She wanted to banish that thought right along with the attraction she still felt toward Logan every time she got anywhere near him. But no matter how hard she tried, she knew she was losing that war on both fronts.

"Skyler?"

When Logan got no answer, he walked toward the front door and looked out the screen. Her car was still there, so at least she hadn't made a run for it while he'd been in the shower. Of course, if she'd known he'd spent those few minutes fantasizing about her joining him, she might have fled the premises as fast as she could.

When he didn't find her on the porch, he walked down the hallway until he reached her old bedroom. She lay on her side, curled into the fetal position on her childhood bed. He wanted nothing more in that moment than to join her there, but not for sex. All he wanted was to cradle her in his arms, to keep away whatever memory plagued her here. Instead, he turned and left her to her rest. As he put together sandwiches and pulled out a new bag of chips, he thought back to how worried she'd looked when she'd found him sitting at the back of the ambulance earlier.

She would never admit it and might not even realize it, but there had been something in her eyes that said she cared. The thought occurred to him that he ought to be freaked out and planning his escape, but he wasn't. As odd as it might seem, he liked the idea of someone caring about him.

Should he allow her to care when he wasn't sure how long he was staying? His conscience told him it wasn't fair to her, even if he didn't plan to totally disappear from her life. The last thing he wanted to do was hurt her, but he knew it would be hard to fight the attraction he felt toward her. It wouldn't even give him peace when he slept.

When he had the food ready, he took it in a cooler out onto the porch. He sat in the swing and watched the end of another day approaching. As he gently swung back and forth, he listened to the quiet and was amazed it didn't have him running for his truck and the open road.

He'd been outside about an hour when the sound of footsteps made him look toward the screen door as it opened.

Skyler smoothed her hair as she stepped out onto the porch. "You should have woken me up."

"You looked like you were resting so well I didn't want to disturb you."

She walked to the edge of the porch and looked west, toward the last hint of the orange sunset disappearing into the deepening purple. "It's always so beautiful out here this time of day."

"Can't argue with that."

She turned and leaned back against the porch support, facing him. "You look a little less like a chimney sweep than earlier."

"Amazing what running water and a little soap will do." He patted the swing beside him.

Skyler hesitated, and he could almost see the argument going on in her head. She was most likely the smarter, more sensible of the two of them. But when he looked at her, he didn't want to be smart or sensible. He wanted to give his desire free rein.

"I don't bite," he said. "Unless, of course, you want me to."

She snorted at that and came to sit beside him.

He leaned over and retrieved her sandwich, bottle of water and the bag of chips.

She accepted the sandwich and took a bite. They ate in silence for a few minutes.

"How long has it been since you lived out here?" he asked.

Though he wasn't touching her, he sensed a slight stiffening of her posture.

"Since I went to college. I'd come back for breaks, but I

never lived here again full-time." She paused for a couple of heartbeats. "My mom died while I was in school in Austin."

"I'm sorry."

"Me, too."

"What about your dad?"

"A couple of months after that," she said, a definite catch in her words.

"I didn't mean to bring up bad memories."

"It's not you. Just being here is enough for that to happen."

"So that's why you want to sell it?"

"That, and I could use the money to invest in the expansion of the park, and..."

"The baby."

She nodded and took a drink of her water. "What about you? You said you grew up on a ranch."

"In the middle-of-nowhere, North Dakota."

"Your parents still alive?"

"Yeah. They still live on the same ranch. And all my brothers and sisters live in the same county. They're not what you'd call adventurous."

"You must have gotten all those genes in your family."

"You could say that." He took a swig of his beer.

"Sorry."

He glanced at Skyler in the dimming light. Damn, she was beautiful. "What for?"

"I didn't mean to hit a sore subject."

"What makes you say that?"

"It was obvious—the look on your face, the way you tensed and looked like you were going to crush your bottle."

He shrugged. "Just one of those things you can't change." He considered the wisdom of telling her everything, but he decided to trust her, that she would eventually see that his past didn't mean he was going to be some deadbeat dad. "My parents, my entire family except for Jesse and his parents, don't get me at all. They can't understand why anyone would ever want to leave North Dakota, let alone travel all over the country. They never let me go anywhere as a kid. I thought I was going to suffocate before I got old enough to leave."

"So that's why you don't stay in one place for very long, why you're always on the go?"

"Yeah. From the day I left, I've tried any crazy thing I've come across just to say I've done it."

"I can't imagine living like that."

"You never know, you might like it. After all, you didn't think you'd like skydiving either."

"A once-in-a-lifetime thing is different than constantly living on the edge. There's something to be said for stability and roots, building something that will last."

Yeah, they were boring. Luckily, he didn't say the words. And a part of him wondered if that was the younger version of him thinking them. When he noted the change in the air surrounding them, he realized by his not agreeing with her that he'd strengthened her belief that he would forever be a wanderer.

"You're right," he said. "I've been thinking about sticking around, giving Blue Falls a try."

"I don't want you to stay out of some sense of obligation."

He sensed something she left unsaid. Did she want him to stay for some other reason? Could he do it? He hated that he couldn't answer that question with any certainty.

She stood and headed for the steps.

He jumped to his feet and hurried to place himself between her and her avenue of escape. "Don't go." He reached up and slid a lock of her hair behind her ear.

"Logan, don't. I'm not the kind of girl you want."

"I don't know about that. I'd say I'm wanting you quite a bit right now."

"You want sex, and our one night together to the contrary,

that's not what I'm looking for. I have roots here, a business, stability, and someday I want a husband and brothers and sisters for this baby." She placed her hand lovingly on her stomach. "I'm the exact thing you ran away from. The only reason you keep chasing me is because I keep saying no. If I were suddenly to say yes, it wouldn't take long before you realized I'm your worst nightmare, that I'm boring."

"You could never be boring."

"Well, before long I'm going to be fat and no doubt even grumpier than I am now."

"You'll still be beautiful."

She gave him a sad smile. "You're welcome to stay here as long as you like. Don't feel like you have to do anything else. You did enough today by saving the house. You have a life, same as I do."

"Skyler." He started to caress her face, but she stepped out of his reach.

"Goodbye, Logan."

Those words echoed inside him long after she'd driven away and disappeared into the night. As he stood in the darkness, he didn't think he'd ever felt so alone. So empty.

Chapter Twelve

The nap she'd taken in her old bedroom proved to be the best sleep Skyler got all night. When she'd tried to go to sleep in her own bed, she couldn't quiet her mind enough to relax. She kept fantasizing about what life would be like if Logan could quit his nomadic ways and make a life in Blue Falls. She told herself she'd be satisfied if they could simply raise their child together, but that was a lie. She liked Logan, liked him a lot. And though she was probably setting herself up for heartache, she allowed herself to also dream about giving in to his flirtations and making love to him again.

After she'd left the ranch the previous night, she'd felt more alone than she had before she'd met him. Even all her common-sense arguments against getting too attached were weakening.

Knowing she wouldn't be able to concentrate on work this morning, she instead headed out to do some shopping. As she filled her cart with everyday items like toilet paper and the chocolate pudding cups she'd been craving lately, she thought about how Logan never had to buy normal things like cookware or shower cleaner. When you lived in motel rooms and ate at restaurants or out of coolers, someone else took care of those things.

She turned down another aisle and found herself next to the baby section. Even though she should give it a wide berth until she'd made it known she was pregnant, she couldn't seem to resist the pull. The next thing she knew, she was in the midst of the adorable little outfits. Being surrounded by that much cuteness was a little like getting a sugar rush from eating too many cookies.

A little yellow-and-white dress covered with daisies caught her eye. It came with a set of ruffly underpants and a hat. The fabric was so soft that she wanted to rub it against her cheek.

She placed her hand over her stomach, trying to imagine what she would look like in the months ahead as her body changed to accommodate the life inside her.

"What do you think, sweet pea?" she said low where no one could hear her. "You like this one?"

Movement out of the corner of her eye startled Skyler. When she turned in that direction, she saw Logan staring back at her with an expression that looked as if his brain was in the process of short-circuiting. She bit her lip to keep it from trembling because he looked like a man who'd been smacked upside the head with reality and didn't know how to deal with it.

"Hey," she managed to say as she placed the dress back on the rack.

"Hey." He appeared to mentally shake himself free of his temporary deer-in-headlights moment. "How are you?"

He sounded so distant. More than at any time since she'd met him, she wanted him to tease her, toss out some flirty comment as only he could. Instead, he glanced toward the front of the store as if estimating how long it would take him to reach the exit. When he shifted his gaze again, it landed on the little dress. "Are you having a girl?"

"It's too early to tell." Fearing that lingering in the baby section with Logan would set tongues to wagging, she moved away from the racks of clothes, crossing the aisle to stand next to a display of greeting cards. Before she could talk herself out of it, she turned back toward Logan. "Would you like to come over for lunch?"

She expected a quick yes, so when Logan shook his head, her heart sank.

"I'd best make the most of the daylight to work."

What he said made sense, but she knew there was more to it. He was already pulling away, and she didn't know if it was inevitable or if she'd finally pushed him away one too many times.

"Oh, okay." It was on her lips to suggest dinner instead, but the words would go no farther.

He met her eyes again. "Thanks for the offer, though." He paused for a moment. "Are you really okay, after everything that happened yesterday?"

She nodded and managed a smile. "Just as long as you don't decide to battle a pack of wild dogs today."

He smiled at that, but it wasn't the type of full-of-life, infectious smile she was used to from him. She tried not to read too much into it, telling herself that his reaction to seeing her with baby clothes was normal for a new father-to-be. After all, didn't she regularly face some new aspect of her pregnancy that struck her dumb?

"Well, I better get going," Logan said.

She nodded and told herself not to watch as he walked away. She didn't last two seconds, and it took all her willpower to not run after him as he headed out the front door.

ALL THE WAY back to the ranch, Logan tried to shake off the edgy, freaked-out feeling that had hit him the moment he saw Skyler holding that tiny dress. He thought he'd come to terms with impending fatherhood, but it punched him right in the gut imagining a little girl of his in that dress. God, he couldn't be a father. He had to be the most ill-suited person in the world for that role.

But there was no going back now. He had to pull himself together and deal.

When he reached the ranch, he immersed himself in work, hoping the panicked feeling would take a hike. He worked hard and long enough that he should have fallen asleep as soon as he hit the pillow late that night. Instead, he stared at the ceiling thinking about the enormity of the fact that he had helped create a child. The thought kept looping over and over in his mind even as he eventually started to fall asleep in the wee hours.

Logan had no idea how much time had passed when he jerked awake, panting from a dream that had seemed so real that his heart still raced as if it was being chased by an ax murderer. He'd been trying to leave Blue Falls, but roots from the ground had surrounded his truck, overtaking it, breaking out the windows in order to get him. They'd invaded the cab of the truck and snaked around his arms, his legs, his entire body, eventually covering even his face, smothering him.

He threw off the sheet that lay over him and sat on the side of the bed. A glance at his phone revealed it was after two in the morning. But a bright moon cast the land outside in a blue-white glow. Skyler was right. He wasn't cut out for this domestic stay-in-one-place crap. He had to get out of here. He tried to make himself feel better by telling himself it was for the best to go now before he really hurt Skyler. He would send her money, come visit, help her anytime she asked, but if he didn't get back on the road soon, he feared he might smother.

He stood and started tossing his few belongings in his bag. Within five minutes he was driving away from the house. It wasn't the first time he'd taken to the road in the middle of the night, and it likely wouldn't be the last.

He was halfway to Dallas before he realized Skyler's house key was still in his pocket. But he wasn't turning back. For the first time in his life, he felt ashamed of running away.

SKYLER KNEW WHAT was in the envelope even before the house key slid out onto her palm. She opened the single sheet of paper. Scrawled across it were only two words. *I'm sorry.* Logan hadn't even signed it, not that there was any need. Irrational tears pooled in her eyes. She'd known he would leave, had even tried convincing herself that's what she wanted, so why was she on the verge of crying?

Stupid pregnancy hormones, that had to be it. It certainly was not because she could honestly visualize any sort of life together with him. She barely knew the man. Just because he was the biological father of her child didn't mean he had to be a part of their lives. And it looked as though he wouldn't be.

She batted away the tears and focused on work. If she had any hope of selling the ranch and getting the park projects under way before she got so big all she could think of was her hurting feet, she had to find someone else to finish the repairs to the ranch property. But not today. A small writers' conference was coming into the inn, she had two meetings with food vendors and she was supposed to meet Elissa later to attend the opening of a new exhibit at Merline Teague's art gallery.

While part of her wanted to just curl up on her couch with a carton of ice cream and an afternoon of her favorite movies, she knew keeping busy was actually better. She needed the work to keep her mind off of Logan until the memory of him started to fade.

She managed to forget about Logan for short stretches, but the moment she got off a phone call or left a meeting the image of him was right there in the front of her mind again. If they'd just had that one night together and she'd never seen him again, would she have already begun to forget him? Was it only the fact that she was going to have a living, breathing tie to him for the rest of her life that kept her remembering his face, wondering where he was, what he was doing?

A little part of her that had nothing to do with common

sense whispered "No" and she was afraid it was right. After all, remembering how his hands felt as they skimmed along her skin, his lips capturing hers, the way her body had come alive as he'd made love to her, had nothing to do with raising a child.

As she got ready for the art opening, she couldn't keep her mind from reliving all her moments with Logan. The pizza and the flowers, dancing with him at the music hall and then again at India's wedding, the sight of him covered in soot after he'd battled a blaze alone to save her childhood home. But that was all they were, memories. He'd come back before because he'd wanted a repeat of their night together. This time she had no doubt he was gone for good.

When she reached the gallery, Merline Teague greeted her at the door and gave her a kiss on the cheek. "You're looking lovely tonight, dear," Merline said. "Did you do something new with your hair or makeup?"

Skyler shook her head. "No."

Merline looked at her a moment longer, as if she couldn't quite pinpoint what was different. A jolt went through Skyler. Could people tell merely by looking at her, even this early, that she was pregnant? She'd heard of a pregnancy glow, but she would have bet money that her look was more baggy eyes and a faint tinge of green.

Merline, thankfully, shifted her attention to the next arrival, allowing Skyler to make her escape into the milling crowd. She found Elissa and Verona talking in a back corner and headed that way.

"Isn't this adorable?" Verona said as she took a step closer to the artwork hanging on the display wall.

Skyler had to agree. The artist had a talent for capturing the sweetness of baby animals, and the bunny depicted in the piece in front of them was darling. Skyler had a vision of it hanging in her baby's nursery.

"I was beginning to wonder if you'd bailed on us," Elissa said when she noticed Skyler.

"No, had a meeting with a vendor who was a little on the chatty side."

A waitress came by with a tray of champagne. Verona and Elissa each took a glass, but Skyler shook her head. "I'm fine, thank you."

When she looked back toward her friends, Verona had an expression on her face that made Skyler want to squirm. The woman was entirely too observant.

Despite everything that was going on in her life and the way Verona kept watching her, Skyler had a nice time visiting with friends and neighbors. After talking to the artist, a young woman from Gruene, Skyler decided to buy the bunny painting.

"He looks like he could just hop off the canvas into your lap, doesn't he?" Verona walked out of the gallery alongside Skyler.

For the first time in her life, being alone with Verona made her truly nervous. She glanced back to see Elissa saying goodbye to Merline and her daughters-in-law, Grace and Brooke.

"It'll look good in a child's room."

Skyler jerked her attention back to Verona before she could think about what that might reveal. But there was no sense denying it. Verona had figured out her secret.

"It's Logan's, isn't it?"

Skyler glanced around them but saw no one nearby. "Yes."

"This is wonderful, dear. I take it you haven't told him, but I bet he'll be excited."

"You would be wrong." Skyler heard the hurt in her voice the same moment Verona did. She hadn't meant to sound like that.

"He's not happy?"

"The fact that he left town without even saying goodbye

indicates no." An inner voice told her that wasn't entirely fair. She believed he'd tried to stay. It just wasn't in him to hang around in one place for long.

Verona grasped Skyler's hand with both of hers. "Oh, honey, I'm so sorry. I was so sure he was a good man."

"I didn't say he was a bad one. I can't exactly blame him for running away from something he didn't plan."

"That's no excuse for shirking his responsibility."

"It's not his responsibility." It was hers and hers alone.

"It most certainly is. You didn't exactly get yourself pregnant."

"Verona, lay off," Elissa said as she walked up to them. "You're not making this any easier."

Verona took a deep breath, then squeezed Skyler's hand. "I'm sorry, sweetie. Don't you worry about anything. We'll get you through this." She looked down at where her hand clasped Skyler's. "I'm so sorry."

"For what?" Skyler wasn't used to hearing Verona be anything other than upbeat.

"For pushing you toward Logan."

"This isn't on you. I made my own decisions." And that fateful decision to go with Logan back to his motel room had changed her life forever.

LOGAN PAID FOR his beer and wandered into the barn that had been turned into a makeshift dance floor for the night. He didn't feel much like dancing or socializing, but it was marginally better than going back to his crap motel and stewing in his thoughts.

Ever since he'd left Blue Falls three weeks ago, he'd ridden as if he'd never even seen a bull. Maybe it was the universe's way of paying him back for running away from Blue Falls without even having the decency to tell Skyler to her face he was leaving.

Judging by how fast he'd left town, she was better off without him. Even as he thought it, something didn't sit well inside him.

He spotted Sam Hall sitting on a bale of hay watching the dancers and tapping the toe of his boot to the music. Only he was a little off the beat. Logan wondered how many beers Sam had had.

"Hey, Logan," Sam said as Logan approached the older bronc rider. "Tough ride tonight."

"I've had better." Hell, he'd had better when he'd first started. "How'd you do?"

"About as well as you did. Guess I'm so old I should hang it up, but I don't know what I'd do with myself otherwise. Probably drink myself to death."

Logan had never really thought about it, but he realized that Sam wasn't married. As he went back through his years of crossing paths with the man, he couldn't remember Sam ever being married. Not that it was a surprise. There were a lot of divorced or single-by-choice guys on the circuit, including him.

"He's a cute little bug," Sam said as he motioned with his bottle toward a little boy dressed just like his dad, one of the team-roping guys Logan didn't know very well. "Phil dotes on that boy." Sam shook his head slowly. "Can't imagine what that's like."

"Having a kid?"

"Nah, I probably got a few of those around somewhere. Having a dad, that's the great mystery. Never knew who my old man was. I used to like to imagine he was some famous actor or a Texas Ranger or something, but he was probably just some loser."

Sam took another swig of his beer as Logan watched Phil with his son. He wondered if Skyler was carrying a boy or a girl. For a moment, he imagined teaching the kid to ride a horse, taking him to rodeos.

"Yep, that boy will grow up right," Sam said, beginning to slur his words a little. He'd probably been drinking like a sponge since the moment his event was over. He looked at Logan, a little glassy-eyed. "How about you? You know your old man?"

"Yeah." Logan took a drink of his own beer to wet the dryness invading his throat.

"Bet you didn't get in as much trouble as I did. I was mad at the world and didn't care who knew it. If it weren't for rodeo, I'd probably be in prison. Not that I've not seen my share of the inside of jail cells."

Why wouldn't the man stop talking? Logan couldn't stand chatty drunks. When a woman half Sam's age caught his eye and he nearly toppled off his hay bale in an effort to pinch her butt, Logan made his escape.

"Hey there, Logan. Don't you owe me a dance?" Amy Fitzwater, the daughter of one of the stockmen, moved close to him and placed her hands against his chest.

How many times in the past had he taken advantage of situations like this, women more than willing to press their bodies against his? Tonight it felt wrong, and he stepped away from her. "Sorry, Amy. I was just leaving."

She gave him a pout meant to change his mind, but it didn't work. He tossed his barely touched beer in the trash on his way out of the barn. He didn't slow down until he got to his truck. He braced his hands against the side of the bed and looked up at the wide expanse of Wyoming sky sprinkled with stars. He wondered if Skyler was looking up at those same stars. Despite her determination that she would be fine on her own, could she be scared deep down? Because as he considered his next move, he sure as hell was.

Could he do it, return to Blue Falls and try to be a father

to his child? The thought of staying in one place still made him jittery, as though if he went back, he'd never be able to escape again. But he couldn't let Skyler face this alone either, no matter her assertions that she could and the groveling he was going to have to do to earn her forgiveness. And the thought of becoming like Sam or the man's father turned his stomach. His kid wasn't going to grow up wondering if his father was a criminal or why he wasn't good enough for his dad to stick around. And he sure didn't want his son or daughter to end up alone and broken like Sam.

With the way he left, Skyler might be less than happy to see him. But he'd deal with that when he got there, because he was going to be a part of his child's life. Knowing he wasn't going to sleep a wink anytime soon, he got into his truck and started driving toward Texas.

Chapter Thirteen

Skyler had just propped up her tired, aching feet when some-one knocked on the door. She sighed and thought about ig-noring it. Who could it be at this time of night, anyway? By ten o'clock most of the guests were either in their rooms or finishing up a late dinner in the dining room. And if it was a member of the staff, they would call her.

With a sigh, she forced herself up off the couch and across her small living area. But when she looked out the peephole, all she could see was what looked like cellophane covering something. What the heck?

When she opened the door, the item she'd seen turned out to be a large gift basket. She spotted a blue teddy bear and a tiny pair of socks. Gradually, whoever was holding the bas-ket started to lower it.

Her breath caught and she gripped the edge of her door to steady herself. "Logan. What are you doing here?"

"Bringing you a Texas-sized gift basket." He smiled that resistance-melting smile that had led her off the path of san-ity and into his bed.

It wasn't going to work again. She'd told everyone, includ-ing herself, that she'd been fine with him leaving. But now that he stood in front of her, a flood of emotions welled up within her. Anger, betrayal and the need to hurt him.

"You have to leave." She started to shut the door in his face.

Logan put his hand against the door, balancing the large basket in his other hand. "I'm sorry, Skyler."

"So you said in your note."

"You have every right to be mad at me."

"Yes, I do."

"Can we please just talk?"

"We don't have anything to talk about. You made your feelings abundantly clear."

Logan let out a long breath, and she realized that he looked tired, really tired. But she couldn't let that soften her toward him. She wasn't exactly bursting with energy at the moment either.

"I made a mistake, a huge one," he said. "One I want to correct."

"Pretty sure that boat has sailed."

"I'm going to be here for you, for the baby. I've given you every reason not to believe me, but I swear I'll prove it to you."

Skyler sighed, wanting this conversation to be over. "For how long? A day? A week? Maybe you'll even make it a month. But what happens when you start feeling trapped again?"

"It can't be any worse than how I've felt since I left. Not an hour has gone by without me thinking about you, about how immature and selfish it was of me to just drive away."

She searched his eyes, looking for a lie, but she didn't see one. "I want to believe you, but I just can't."

Logan sat the basket down, then met her gaze. "You don't now, but you will."

This time when he walked away, she couldn't watch.

"You have to admit, there's a lot of great stuff in here," India said as she picked through all the items in the basket Logan had left the night before.

"It's going to take more than a few presents to make me believe that particular tiger has changed his stripes."

"You didn't think you'd ever see him again, and yet here he is back in town."

"Which seems to be a pattern with him."

"I say take whatever he's willing to give but don't bank on anything," Elissa said.

Skyler caught the irritated look India shot Elissa. India's newfound happiness obviously made her want everyone around her to be happy, too.

"It would be easier if he just stayed away altogether."

India came to sit beside Skyler on the couch. "Is there something there between the two of you?"

Skyler laughed. "You're kidding, right?"

"Not at all. After he left, you seemed so sad. You tried to hide it, but I know you too well."

"I wasn't sad. I was tired."

India seemed as if she wanted to say something else, but she refrained at the last moment. It was enough, however, to make Skyler uncomfortable. The truth was a part of her was still, after everything, very much attracted to Logan. She had to keep reminding herself it was only physical, nothing more. But then her traitorous memory would snap to the picnic, the flowers, the day of the fire and tempt her to believe in him. To admit it was more than physical, at least on her part.

But she couldn't. He'd left her and their baby behind, and chances were he'd do it again. She wasn't about to even think about opening up her heart to someone, giving him the ammunition to crush it. She'd seen that happen with her parents, and she had no desire to walk down the same path her mother had taken.

"What are you going to do if he does stick around?" Elissa asked.

"Ignore him until he goes away."

That proved difficult when she walked into the dining room a few minutes later to see him sitting at a table right next to the beverage station.

"Good morning, Skyler."

She considered turning around without acknowledging him, but that would just make him more determined. He'd once admitted to her that he liked the chase. "Morning." She poured a glass of milk and walked back out the door.

She expected Logan to follow her, but he didn't. And the longer she sat in her office, glancing up at the doorway, the more irritated she got at herself for letting his mere presence under the same roof bother her.

Of course, it was when she'd finally settled down enough to work that he appeared at the door.

"I'm going to need the key to the house back."

She just stared at him.

"I left work unfinished, so I thought I'd get back to it today."

"I'm in the process of hiring someone else, someone dependable this time." He didn't have to know that all she'd managed to do was think about it.

"No sense paying for the labor when you can get it for free."

"Because that worked out so well last time."

"So you don't believe in second chances?"

"If I say no, will you go away?"

"Nope." He smiled, and it caused that fluttery feeling in her chest. Why couldn't he turn butt ugly overnight?

"Fine." Anything to make him leave her in peace. She pulled open the desk drawer where she'd stashed the key, but she didn't let him see that she'd kept the envelope it had arrived in. She wasn't even sure why she had. She extended the key to him.

He stepped into the office, making it seem much smaller.

"Thank you. Hopefully I won't almost burn to a crisp this time."

She didn't respond. In all honesty, she didn't know how. This man was very, very good at scrambling her thoughts and emotions, and she hated that feeling of not being in control of either.

Something passed over his face, there one moment and gone the next. If she didn't know better, she'd swear it was disappointment. Well, what did he expect from her, effusive thanks?

"I'll get to it, then. Have a nice day."

He was already gone when she found herself saying, "You, too."

LOGAN STOOD IN front of the ranch house. The work that needed to be done here was nothing compared to what he evidently was going to have to do to get back into Skyler's good graces. But he was oddly prepared to do whatever it took. He didn't totally understand his new, deeper determination to make her believe in him, but it was there nonetheless. So he went with it.

He didn't bother Skyler for the next few days, instead staying at the ranch and working from early morning until he fell into bed at night. By the end of the week, the place was beginning to look inviting again. All of the fencing was fixed, the rotten boards on the house replaced, weeds ripped away and a new kitchen faucet installed. Before he got started stripping away the old paint on the house, he poured an entire bottle of water over his head and used a bandanna to wipe off his face.

The sun beat down mercilessly as he worked throughout the afternoon, but he was proud of how much he got done by the time the sun started to set. He wanted to call Skyler and have her come out to see his progress, but he suspected she wouldn't budge from her little safe haven. He'd really messed up by leaving before.

As he sat on the lowered tailgate of his truck, he thought maybe he should wait until he was completely done with the renovations before he invited her out. Maybe she'd be more impressed, more willing to believe that he did want to help her.

He dragged his tired, aching body inside to the kitchen. But when he looked in the fridge, he couldn't face another ham-and-cheese sandwich. Half of him just wanted to go collapse in the bed, but the other half managed to trudge to the shower. After he dressed in clean clothes, he headed into town.

He glanced at the Wildflower Inn as he passed it as if Skyler might happen to be outside where he could see her. She was nowhere to be seen, which caused an unexpected pang in his middle. Convincing himself it was hunger, he drove on into downtown. He'd aimed to go to the Primrose, but another idea hit him. Several minutes later he walked out of Gino's with a piping-hot pepperoni pizza.

Next he stopped at the Mehlerhaus Bakery, where a lovely Hispanic woman moved to the counter to help him.

"I'll take one of every kind of cupcake you have."

With pizza and cupcakes in hand, he headed straight for the inn. He didn't even pause in the lobby on the way to Skyler's apartment. He knocked. "Pizza delivery."

It wasn't Skyler who opened the door. Instead, it was Elissa. She took the pizza from him.

"Thanks. I was getting hungry." And then she shut the door in his face.

He stood there staring at the door, stunned into inaction. Before he could decide what to do next, the door opened again. This time it was Skyler.

"I'm sorry about that," she said.

He smiled. "You're being nice to me."

"I'm being civil. Is there something wrong at the ranch? A swarm of locusts hasn't descended, has it?"

"No, it remains plague- and fire-free." At the expectant look on her face, he went on. "I just thought we could talk."

"About?"

"The baby, how you're doing."

"I have company."

The door opened wider behind her, and India ushered an obviously irritated Elissa out the door, passing between Skyler and Logan. "We were just leaving," India said.

"You got here like five minutes ago," Skyler said, sounding a little desperate at her friends' departure.

"See you tomorrow," India said over her shoulder.

Skyler sagged against the doorframe. "Do I have one of those faces that says 'Please abandon me in my hour of need'?"

Logan felt the sting of that as if she'd hit him with a whip. "Maybe they thought we had things to talk about."

For a long moment, Skyler simply stared at him. He felt a bit as if he were being dissected. When she finally opened the door wider for him to come inside, he almost couldn't believe it.

Her apartment wasn't as big as he'd imagined it, but she really didn't need much space for one person. Of course, in a few months there would be two. As he followed her, she paused to straighten a blocky candleholder that hadn't looked the least bit out of place.

"Nice place," he said.

"Probably better than that old ranch house."

"I don't mind it."

She rounded the end of the small dining room table where the pizza sat and braced her hands against the back of a chair. "You haven't fled in the night yet. That's a good sign."

He wondered if she was ever going to let him live that

down. "No. It's actually felt good to be back at the ranch. Last night I sat out on the porch and saw several shooting stars."

"Good. Maybe someone else will be as charmed as you seem to be and snatch it up. That would certainly be one less headache in my life."

"Is that how you see me, as a headache?"

She looked startled by his question. "I didn't say that. You're...unexpected."

"And you don't like unexpected."

"For the most part, no."

"So you don't like surprises?"

"Not particularly. I've not had a good track record with them." She pulled out the chair she was grasping. "You might as well help me eat this pizza. I already feel like I'm eating enough to feed half of Texas. Before long I'll be that big, too."

"So I should take these back?" He held up the bakery box.

"Tell me you didn't."

He opened the lid and playfully fanned the box in front of her. "What? Bring you delicious cupcakes? I didn't. These are a figment of your imagination."

"I hope you planned to share those with everyone staying at the inn."

"I didn't know which was your favorite, so I bought one of each."

"You are evil," she said as she reached inside and grabbed the chocolate cupcake.

"You haven't eaten your pizza yet."

"I stopped having to follow that 'dessert comes last' rule the day I went to college."

He laughed and felt a weight lift off his shoulders, one he hadn't been aware he was carrying.

"Hey, I like how you think." He grabbed a vanilla cupcake and took a huge bite, getting cream-cheese frosting on his nose.

Skyler laughed. He loved the sound of her laughter, and he wanted to tell her how beautiful she was when she smiled. But she would probably clam up, robbing him of the light feeling in his chest. And she needed to laugh more. He realized how often she looked stressed out or upset. That couldn't be good for the baby.

He lifted his cupcake. "I bet every man in Blue Falls is after the woman who makes these."

"They better not be, because she's married to the sheriff."

"Drat, all the good ones are taken."

He watched her closely for her reaction, and he caught a brief smile. Was she finally thawing toward him?

"How are you feeling?"

"You ask that a lot."

"Maybe I just want to make sure you're okay."

Skyler placed what remained of her cupcake down on a napkin. "I'm tired, but that's to be expected."

"And your doctor says everything is fine?"

"I'm healthy. So is the baby." She looked across the table at him. "You think it's going to be a boy." It wasn't a question.

"Why do you say that?"

"Maybe because everything in the basket you gave me was blue."

"I didn't really think about it. I just went through the store grabbing whatever looked like something you could use."

"You put the basket together yourself?" She seemed genuinely surprised.

"I picked all the things in it, but they had a basket-making service. It was one of those superstores full to the rafters with baby stuff. I felt like if I'd stayed in there five more minutes, I would have walked out pregnant."

Skyler snorted, then covered her nose and mouth for a moment in embarrassment. "That would certainly be the end to your bull-riding career."

They finished off their cupcakes, and the silence wasn't as awkward as it could have been. "So, when can we find out what the baby is?"

"Not for two or three more months."

His cupcake history, he opened the pizza box and inhaled the heavenly aroma of bread and Italian spices. "Is there anything I can do to help you out?"

"Stop bringing me things to make me fat."

He laughed a little. "Seriously."

"No. Well, nothing beyond the ranch repairs. I need to sell the place so I can stop thinking about it, and hopefully the repairs will up my chances of that."

Something about her answer made him think it wasn't as simple as she tried to make it seem. "Why does the place hurt you so much?"

He thought she might not share whatever old hurt was lurking there behind her eyes, but then she sighed and leaned back. "There's a reason I don't trust you to not leave again. I see a lot of my father in you."

"He was a rodeo rider?"

"No, but he had incurable wanderlust. I don't doubt that he loved my mom and me, but it just wasn't enough to keep him at home. He tried, but the call of some new adventure or another always pulled him away. I grew up not knowing when or if I would ever see my father again. And as I got older, I began to hate him for it, more because of how I could see my mom's heartache every time he left, how she would watch the road as if she could bring him home with just the power of her thoughts. But it never worked. He came home, then he left again in a never-ending cycle.

"The ranch had been his idea, but it was Mom who kept it going while he was off chasing some new pot of gold at the end of the rainbow. She worked herself to death. I never hated my father so much as when he showed up for her funeral. Somehow I made it through the service and the burial, but I lost it the moment we got back to the ranch. I screamed at him that he'd been the one to kill her as surely as if he'd put a bullet in her head. A couple of months later he went off the road and hit a tree. He wasn't wearing a seat belt and was thrown from the truck. The officer said he looked like he'd been crying, and I'll wonder for the rest of my life if it was because of Mom or because of what I said."

Logan slid his hand across the table and captured hers. She was so lost in her painful past that she let him. "I'm sorry, Skyler. I truly am."

"It's not your fault."

"But bringing up those memories was. I'm sorry for that."

She nodded, then met his gaze. "What really made you come back?"

He risked telling her the truth about his conversation with Sam. "The longer he talked, the worse I felt. I don't want any child of mine not knowing who I am or growing up hating me because I'm the world's worst dad. I want to be there, be the cool dad."

Skyler stared at him for several seconds without saying anything. Finally, he couldn't stand it anymore. "What are you thinking?"

"I want to believe you. Really, I do."

"But you don't."

"I'm sorry. I've just seen good intentions fall by the way-side too often."

He couldn't argue her doubt, because her father wasn't the only person who'd reinforced it. All he could do was prove himself to her one day at a time. And as he looked at the beautiful woman across from him, he realized that he didn't want her trust just because of the child she was carrying. He wanted very much to have Skyler believe in him, to know in her heart he'd be there for her whenever she needed him, for whatever reason.

As he left a few minutes later, plans were already spinning in his head, ones that would make Skyler look at him with something other than the expectation that he would leave again at any moment. She'd been left alone too much, and no matter how hard it might be for him to change his ways, he wasn't about to add to her mountain of pain.

Chapter Fourteen

Logan stepped out of the hardware store and nearly ran into Liam Parrish.

"Hey," Liam said as he eyed the buckets of paint in Logan's hands. "Looks like you're still busy fixing up Skyler's old place."

"Yeah. Lots to do."

"You got time to ride in this weekend's rodeo? We've got room for a few more riders."

Logan started to say no, that he was busy, but then the itch started. He hadn't let himself think about it since he'd come back to Blue Falls, afraid it would make him break his word to Skyler, but he missed being around a rodeo. Maybe if he rode in the local event, it would take the edge off.

"Sure, sign me up."

"Great. Try to stay cool. It's gonna be another scorcher today."

Liam stepped inside the store, and Logan turned to head for his truck. A flyer in the window caught his eye. He stepped closer so he could read it.

"To celebrate the reopening of Wren Cove Park, join us for a community canoe outing on the lake."

Logan noted the date and time, then smiled.

Hours later he was up on a ladder painting when he heard a vehicle turn off the road. He turned, anticipation leaping as he expected to see Skyler. But it wasn't her car coming toward him. By the time he reached the bottom of the ladder, Elissa was walking toward him.

"What are you doing?" she asked.

Well, hello to you, too. "Painting a house."

"Did Skyler ask you to do that?"

"Not specifically. Our deal was that I could stay here if I made the place more attractive to buyers." He gestured toward the house. "Thus, new paint."

She quirked an eyebrow at him. "What's your game?"

"My game?"

"Yeah, you fly the coop, and then you just magically reappear claiming you're a different man now."

"I never said that. I'm not going to stand here and lie to you and say I don't miss the road and the circuit, because I do. But that doesn't mean I'm going to be some loser who abandons his kid."

"And what about Skyler?"

"I don't plan on abandoning her either."

"That's not what I mean. Do you care about her?"

"Of course I do. She's carrying my child." But it was more than that, wasn't it? Otherwise, he wouldn't think about her approximately a thousand times a day. There was something about her that drew him despite the fact that she was the opposite of every other woman he'd ever been with. She was steady, responsible and practical, and that should have scared him. But it didn't, and he couldn't figure out why. Something deep inside told him it was more than the fact she was as beautiful as a goddess.

"What if there were no child?"

His heart thudded extra hard. "Is something wrong?"

Elissa waved off his concern. "No, Skyler and the baby are fine. What I want to know is how you feel about Skyler aside from the baby."

"I like her." He paused as more realization seemed to click into place inside him. "A lot."

Elissa nodded. "That's what I wanted to hear. You planning on flaking out on her again? Because if you do, you'd better not show your face in this town again. I might be forced to run you down with a delivery truck, and I don't think I'd like prison very much."

"I don't want to hurt her. She's been hurt too much."

Elissa gave him a questioning look.

"She told me about her parents."

Elissa's mouth fell open a little. "She never talks about that."

It made him feel good that Skyler had trusted him enough to tell him something so personal.

Elissa looked toward the house again. "I think you've done more work than Skyler expected. This can't be cheap."

"I've been surprised by how much I've enjoyed working out here. When I think I might be close to done, I see something else that could be improved."

He caught the brief curious look Elissa shot in his direction. "I don't know whether to like you or stay mad at you for your skipping-town stunt."

"I vote for liking me."

Elissa rolled her eyes. "Of course you would."

After Elissa finally left, he finished painting the section of the exterior he'd been working on, then headed toward the barn. With some grunting and tugging, he got the old canoe up on a pair of sawhorses. He skipped going in for dinner as he scrubbed and cleaned, checked it for leaks, and replaced its dulled red paint with a couple coats of purple. As he stood back and eyed his work, he was left with the feeling that something was missing. He thought about painting Skyler's name, but that didn't seem right either.

He didn't know how long he stood there until the perfect

thing hit him out of the blue. He grabbed the smallest brush he had and a little can of white paint. Along the upper edge of the canoe, he painted the words that he felt described Skyler in all her hardworking, determined glory.

"Looks like a good turnout," Verona said as she approached Skyler where she stood at the edge of the park.

"Yeah, way more than I expected. Thanks for putting this together."

"Least I could do after how hard you've worked to get the park usable again."

"Are you going out?"

"Yeah, I'm hitching a ride with Pete. That boy sure is nice."

Skyler smiled because she knew that look. Verona was already cooking up plans to fix Pete up with someone.

"What about you?" Verona asked. "If anyone should be enjoying this, it's you."

Skyler shook her head. "Don't have a canoe."

"Yes, you do."

Skyler's heart leaped at the sound of Logan's voice. She hadn't seen him since the night she'd told him about her parents. She'd half convinced herself that she'd scared him off, but Elissa had said she'd seen him out working at the ranch as she'd driven by with a delivery.

Logan pointed toward his truck, where part of a purple canoe hung out over the open tailgate. "Your chariot awaits."

Verona patted Skyler's arm. "You two have fun." And then she was off with a mischievous smile playing at her lips.

"I don't know if I should do this," Skyler said.

"I promise I won't dump you in the lake."

Damn it, how was she supposed to resist that smile and the lure of watching him paddle them around the lake? A warm, jittery feeling sped through her as she allowed herself to remember some of the daydreams she'd had about him lately.

She knew it was a bad idea, that he could change his mind and leave for good at any moment, but she couldn't seem to help herself. The man drew her like a magnet despite all the reasons why he shouldn't.

She followed him to his truck to look at the canoe. "I doubt this was in your traveling bag."

"No, it was in your barn."

Her breath caught and she took an unsteady step backward. Logan grabbed her as if he thought she might fall.

"Are you okay? Do you need to go inside?"

She shook her head. "No, I'm fine. I...I didn't recognize it."

"What's wrong?"

"Nothing." She paused, staring at the canoe. "It's just that I used to go on canoe rides in this with my dad when I was a little girl. It was so peaceful out on the lake, and I always knew that when we were out there, he couldn't leave me."

Logan cursed under his breath. "I'm sorry. I should have left it alone."

This time she reached out to him and took his hand. "No, it's okay. It was nice of you to fix it up. I like the new color." She spotted writing down the side and tried to read it. "What does that say?"

Logan grabbed the end of the canoe and pulled it far enough out of the truck bed that she could read the words. *The Sky's the limit*.

Her heart performed a little loopdy-loop in her chest. The extra flourish he'd put on *Sky* made it obvious it was a play on her name. When she met his gaze, she saw need there a need for approval.

"I love it."

"It seemed to fit."

She wanted to kiss him right then, take his face in her hands and kiss him until the rest of the world faded away.

And from his expression, she didn't think he'd need much convincing to let her.

"Let me help you with that."

The moment broken, Skyler looked over to see Liam approaching, India and his daughter, Ginny, not far behind.

As the men hefted the canoe and started carrying it toward the water, Ginny ran off to play with some of the other kids. India fell into step beside Skyler.

"You going out with Logan?"

"Yeah, though I probably shouldn't."

"Why not?"

"Because I don't want to start believing in things that may not be possible."

India clasped Skyler's arm and stopped her. "What types of things?"

Skyler glanced at Logan, and her heart ached with longing.

"You're falling for him, aren't you?"

"I don't know. I feel all jittery and unsettled around him, like I have no control over my emotions. It doesn't make any sense."

"It makes perfect sense."

Skyler looked back at her friend. "In what universe?"

"Love doesn't have to make sense. It just is."

"I don't love him. I can't. I don't even really know him."

"How well did I know Liam when I started falling for him? I'd just met him, and something clicked though I fought against it tooth and nail. I know how scary it is when your brain is telling you one thing but your heart is insisting on something else entirely."

"It's probably nothing more than lust. I mean, I did go to bed with the man the day I met him."

"Maybe it is, but maybe it's not. You won't know unless you give yourself permission to find out."

"I don't know if I can."

"I know it's scary to let go. It feels safe to be in control of everything, but it's a lie. Sometimes when you take a chance, it's so worth it."

India's words were still echoing in Skyler's head a few minutes later when she allowed Logan to help her into the canoe. Instead of shoving it the rest of the way into the water, however, he walked away.

"Where are you going?"

"I'll be right back."

What in the world was he doing? When he returned, he had a small cooler in one hand and a straw cowboy hat in the other. He set the cooler in the middle of the canoe, then plopped the hat on her head.

"So you don't burn that pretty face."

She smiled at the compliment, then turned away, afraid it was a smile that revealed too much. Still, she couldn't help stealing glances at him as he pushed them off from the shore. She knew all too well the definition of the muscles hidden beneath the red T-shirt he wore and what lay under the well-worn jeans.

She took up a paddle to give herself something to focus on other than wishing Logan would take off his shirt.

They paddled for several minutes until they were well away from the shore, close to the middle of the lake. Logan lifted his paddle from the water and lay it across his lap.

"There's water and fruit in the cooler, if you want some," he said.

Suddenly parched, she stowed her paddle and retrieved a water and a bag of white grapes. She ate a couple, then held out the bag to him. "You want some?"

"I wouldn't mind if you fed me."

She shook her head at him, but she had to admit that flirty Logan made her insides dance.

"You wouldn't want me to not have enough energy to paddle back to shore, would you? Unless you want to be stranded in the middle of the lake with me."

"You are impossible." But she moved carefully so she wouldn't overturn the canoe until she was within arm's length of him.

"Actually, I'm quite easy," he said as he gave her a look full of enough heat to cause the canoe to burst into flames.

"Behave or I'll eat all these grapes myself."

"I wouldn't mind watching that."

What had gotten into him? She held out a grape, and he made sure his lips grazed her fingers as he took it from her. Heat rocketed along every nerve in her body. She should move back to the opposite end of the canoe, but she fed him a few more grapes instead. When her nerves couldn't stand it anymore, she retreated and looked out across the lake instead. Even without seeing it, she could feel his gaze on her. It made her so hot that she was tempted to jump into the water to cool off.

"I can't remember the last time I went canoeing," he said.

"Not exciting enough for you?"

"I'll admit I tended to go whitewater rafting more often, but this is nice. Peaceful."

"I wouldn't have pegged you for a guy who liked peaceful."

"Me neither, but…I don't know. It's been nice."

He looked genuinely perplexed that the simple joy of a paddle in a canoe or even hard work out on the ranch could bring him pleasure.

"Do you ever go home, back to North Dakota?"

"Not often. It's always stressful. I used to wonder if maybe there had been a mix-up at the hospital and I was really someone else's kid. I didn't know how else to explain why I was so different than everyone else in my family. I've got to wonder if my parents have had that thought cross their minds a few times."

"I'm sure they love you."

"In their way, but they'll never understand me. And no matter how hard I've tried, I can't understand them. They have no curiosity at all. It's like the world outside of where they live doesn't exist."

"Maybe it's just their comfort zone and they're happy there."

"Maybe." He still sounded as if it was one of life's greatest mysteries, right up there with the meaning of the universe.

She tried not to think about how he might eventually come to look at her as he did his parents. Her heart ached at that possibility. This was why she hadn't wanted to open herself up, because she knew if she allowed herself she could really care about Logan, maybe even fall for him.

As she glanced back at him, she realized she was already fighting a losing battle.

LOGAN'S ARMS FELT a little like noodles by the time he'd paddled around the lake for a couple of hours. The sunset on the water was beautiful, but the way the soft glow lit up Skyler's face put the sunset to shame.

She'd started out the trip tense, but she'd gradually relaxed enough to actually enjoy herself. He'd seen her smile more this afternoon than he ever had. She caught him watching her as they headed back toward the dock.

"What? Did I burn despite the hat?"

"No, you look beautiful. And happy."

She glanced out across the water. "I am. Thank you for this."

"Anytime."

When they reached the dock, he hopped out into the shallow water and pulled the canoe partially up the bank. A lot of the other canoers already had their canoes loaded and were enjoying a cookout over by the picnic shelters.

"Oh, that smells good," Skyler said. "I feel like I could eat an entire cow."

"I think that would be a feat, even for a pregnant lady."

He helped her out of the canoe and wrapped her hand around the crook of his arm. He considered it a good sign that she didn't pull away.

Despite her claim of hunger, Skyler only managed one burger before her fatigue started catching up with her. It was written plainly across her lovely face. Without a word, he took her hand and escorted her toward the exterior door to her apartment. Once there, however, he found he didn't want to let her go. But despite their nice afternoon together, he didn't want to push his luck. Still, he didn't relinquish her hand.

"I had a nice time," she said as she looked at the front of his shirt.

"I did, too. I'm glad you agreed to go with me."

She shrugged. "You have your moments."

It wasn't much on the spectrum of compliments, but it was a lot considering how much she'd tried to push him away, how much he'd failed her. He'd take it and be happy. He wanted nothing more than to pull her to him and kiss her long and deep, but he resisted. Instead, he leaned over and kissed her on the cheek.

"Go get some rest." Reluctantly, he let go of her hand and started walking away.

"Logan?"

His heart skipped at the sound of his name on her lips. "Yeah?"

"Liam said you're riding tomorrow night."

"I am. You going to come watch me?" He filled his words with the same flirtation she hadn't seemed to mind earlier.

"I'll be there. It's for a good cause, the animal shelter."

He didn't mind her hesitance to admit she wanted to watch

him ride. It was enough that she'd be there. Maybe with her in the crowd, his string of pitiful rides would be over.

SKYLER TOOK HER seat on the fairground bleachers just as the public-address announcer indicated the start of the first event.

"You come to watch your hottie ride?" Elissa asked next to her.

Skyler scrunched her forehead as she looked at her friend. "I can't figure out if you like Logan or not. One day you do, one day you don't."

"Pot, meet kettle."

Okay, so she'd been a little back-and-forth about her feelings, too. She chose to blame pregnancy hormones and past experience. What was Elissa's excuse?

"He's trying. Got to give the guy credit for that," Elissa said.

It was true. Since his return to Blue Falls, Logan had given her no reason to doubt his conviction to be there for their child. And she was beginning to believe that he cared for her, too. Take the night before. The old Logan would have pressed his advantage and tried to talk her into going to bed with him. The fact that he hadn't had stunned her and oddly made her want to do exactly that. He was giving her space and time, proving he was more observant than she'd ever given him credit for.

She tried to relax and watch the riders compete, but the closer they got to the bull riding, the more anxious she felt.

Elissa leaned toward her. "You okay?"

"Yeah. Sitting here is just uncomfortable." Which was true, but not the reason for her buzzing nerves. If pressed, she wasn't sure she could identify the real reason. Part of her wanted to see Logan ride, but another part, that growing sliver of her that was coming to care for him more than was wise, was nervous at the idea. She couldn't stop thinking about that gash on his chest, how close he'd come to being killed and how much that frightened her.

When the bull riding was announced, Skyler's heart rate kicked up and her hand instinctively went to her stomach and the gentle bump there.

Even though everyone's attention was on the first rider, Skyler's gaze scanned the area behind the chute. She spotted Logan and couldn't look away. Around her she heard the crowd cheer for what must have been a high-scoring ride, but she watched Logan's every move as he made his way up to the chute and climbed onto the back of a restless bull.

"Next up, Logan Bradshaw riding Mad Marvin," the announcer said.

Skyler held her breath as she watched Logan get situated astride the bull, and then he nodded. The gate swung wide, and the bull came out looking as if he was determined to kick the sky. A second had never seemed so incredibly long, and he had to stay on the bull for eight of them.

A bad feeling came over Skyler a moment before Logan went airborne. She gasped, then cried out when his body slammed against the ground so hard she'd swear she could feel it. "Oh, my God," she said, covering her mouth with her hand. *Come on, Logan, move. Get up.*

Tears stung her eyes, but she blinked them back. He was okay. He had to be.

But when several cowboys leaped into the arena to surround him and others made sure the bull left the ring, she started shaking. Elissa put her arm around her as Skyler watched everything as if it were happening in slow motion, a horrible, agonizing pace that made her want to scream for everyone to hurry, to help Logan.

She blinked and then paramedics ran into the arena. Logan still hadn't moved. India turned and took Skyler's hands in hers.

A hush had fallen over the crowd, as if everyone in attendance was holding their breath. The pause, the frightening not knowing, went on forever before Skyler spotted movement. Did she really see his hand move? Had he lifted it on his own?

In the next moment, a couple of cowboys helped Logan to his feet. Skyler was about to cry in relief when she noticed an ambulance backing up to the end of the arena. And Logan looked mighty unsteady as he was helped into the vehicle.

"Oh, God, something's wrong."

Liam hurried up to the end of the bleachers. "They're taking him to the hospital to run some tests."

"But he'll be okay." Skyler didn't want to think of the alternative. She'd never considered the reason her child might grow up with an absent father might be because Logan had died. Her heart seized up at the thought, and not just for her child's sake.

Liam gave her a serious look. "He was out cold for a good bit, and he's still addled. Hopefully it's just a concussion, but they want to make sure."

"I..."

Elissa stood. "We'll take you."

India stood, too, and didn't let go of Skyler's hands until she passed Skyler off to Liam, who helped her down the bleachers to the ground. Her legs shook as if she'd just run a marathon, but her friends were there to steady her.

Skyler's gaze shot to the ambulance as it left the fairgrounds.

Please, God, let him be okay. I promise not to be so mean to him anymore.

By the time Elissa pulled in at the hospital, Logan was already being rolled inside on a stretcher. Skyler hurried into the E.R., Elissa and India close on her heels, but Logan had already been taken to an examining room. Skyler wanted to march back through the doors that separated the waiting area from where they treated patients, but she knew the hospital staff wouldn't allow it. Instead, she continued to stand where she'd stopped, staring at those doors, praying that this was all a precaution and Logan would be fine.

India placed her hand on Skyler's shoulder. "Let's sit down. We probably won't know anything for a bit."

Skyler shook her head. "I can't sit down."

"Can I help you ladies with something?" The nurse on duty at the desk was someone Skyler didn't know, a feat in a town as small as Blue Falls.

Skyler pointed toward the double doors to the right of the desk. "The guy they just brought in, is he okay?"

"Are you family?"

Skyler swallowed. "No." When the nurse looked as if she was going to say something about not being able to tell Skyler anything because of privacy laws, Skyler placed her hand on her stomach. "But we're going to have a baby."

The nurse's expression softened a bit. "They're checking him out. That's all I can say."

Skyler felt like pacing, but she was afraid to move from where she'd stationed herself. As the minutes ticked by, her nerves stretched to a point where she'd swear she could feel them beginning to fray.

Elissa came to stand next to her. "When did you start falling in love with him?"

Skyler's instinct was to deny it, but she had the sudden fear that if she did, he wouldn't make it. It didn't matter that she'd seen him awake and walking before he'd been brought here. Those doors in front of her felt like the gateway to doom. Not so long ago Skyler had been beyond them, worried about her baby. But that wasn't the memory that haunted her now. Her mother had been taken through those doors, and Skyler hadn't been here to will her to live. She wasn't going to make that mistake again.

"I don't know. I'm not even sure if that's what I feel. All I know is that right now the only thing I want is for him to be okay." And she needed to see the proof of it with her own eyes.

She felt near collapse when she finally saw movement beyond the doors. She was halfway to them when Chloe stepped through.

"I heard you were out here," Chloe said as she put her hands in the pockets of her white lab coat.

"Is Logan okay?"

"He knocked his head pretty good, and he's still woozy. But we did tests, and there doesn't appear to be any permanent damage."

"Can I see him?" The words were out of Skyler's mouth before she realized she was speaking.

Chloe glanced at the nurse, who was busy on the phone. "Come on."

Skyler's heart beat faster with each step. She had to remind herself to breathe, that Chloe had said he was fine.

"I'm okay," Logan said before they reached the room he was in.

"Sir, you shouldn't drive or be alone tonight."

Skyler reached the opening in a curtain that revealed Logan sitting on the side of an examination table. He wasn't wearing a shirt, and her breath caught involuntarily at the sight of all that wonderful flesh. She remembered what it had felt like under her hands, and the desire to touch it again washed over her.

"I've been hurt worse than this before. I don't need—"

"Stop arguing," Skyler said, drawing his attention. She shifted her gaze toward the nurse who'd been going toe-to-toe with Logan. "I'll make sure he does what he's supposed to."

The nurse nodded and left the examination area. With a gentle squeeze on Skyler's shoulder, Chloe slipped away, too, leaving Skyler alone with Logan.

"Couldn't stand to stay away from me while I was half-dressed, huh?" Logan gave her a mischievous grin.

Skyler walked forward, grabbed his shirt and shoved it against his chest. "Get dressed."

Logan didn't argue, but he took his sweet time buttoning his shirt. She took a step back to give him some room, though what she really wanted to do was watch his every movement.

"Why are you here?" he finally asked.

"I came to make sure you hadn't knocked your brain loose. After hearing your conversation with the nurse, I'm not sure you didn't. Maybe they should keep you in the hospital overnight."

"I'm okay. I don't know why everyone is making such a big deal out of it." He stood and immediately had to grab the edge of the bed to steady himself.

Skyler crossed the space to him and placed her hand against his chest, as if she could keep him from toppling forward. Even through his shirt, the warmth of him soaked into her hand and spilled through the rest of her body. "That's why."

His gaze caught hers, and an electricity passed between them. She half expected Logan to lower his lips to hers, and she knew she wouldn't push him away.

"So are you going to make me stand here all night?" he asked.

It took her a moment longer to finally force her feet to take a step back. "No, we'll go back to the inn."

"To your apartment."

It wasn't a question, but she nodded, anyway. She took his hand and placed it on her shoulder as she turned to walk out of the exam room. Logan remained remarkably quiet until they reached her apartment.

"You going to be okay?" Elissa asked Skyler as they watched Logan sink onto the couch.

"Yeah."

Elissa gave her a knowing smile, but Skyler chose to ignore it. Logan was here so she could make sure he was okay and didn't hurt himself further, not because she was planning to seduce him. As soon as she had the thought, her entire body heated with the idea of doing exactly that. Instead, she waved Elissa off and shut the door.

When she turned back toward her living room and saw Logan watching her, she wondered what she'd gotten herself into.

"Why did you come to the hospital?" he asked.

"I told you."

"Would you have done the same if one of the other riders had been tossed?"

"No, I don't know them." She took a breath. "And none of them is the father of my child."

"Is that the only reason?"

"What do you want me to say, Logan?"

"The truth."

She threw her hands up and walked toward him. "What, you want me to say that you scared me half to death? That the longer you lay there in the dirt, the more I prayed that you'd be okay?"

Logan's eyes widened in surprise. He obviously hadn't expected the truth he'd asked for.

Her exhaustion finally caught up with her, and she sank onto the couch beside him. "All I could think was how horrible I'd been to you and how if you died, I wouldn't get the chance to apologize."

Logan took her hand in his, and she didn't have the strength to pull away. She didn't want to, because she liked the feel of his ever-present warmth, his rough, manly hand encircling hers. "It wasn't the first time I've been thrown, and it most likely won't be the last."

She looked up into his eyes. "When you were lying there, not moving, you looked dead. I don't think I've ever been so scared in my life."

"Why? You don't even like me."

"That's not true." Afraid she'd revealed more than she was ready to admit, she broke eye contact.

Logan didn't let her get away with it, though. He lifted her chin so that she faced him again. "Have you changed your mind about me?"

"I don't know. Maybe."

He smiled, and she felt that smile sizzling in every nerve ending in her body. Some part of her mind that automatically shifted into self-protection mode urged her to pull away, reminding her that she was exposing herself to potential hurt. She ignored it and lifted her hand to his cheek.

Logan's smile melted away to be replaced with a hungry look that made her heart skip a beat, maybe two. She was too busy looking into his eyes to count. It was different from how he'd looked at her the night they'd spent together. And as impossible as it ought to be, she wanted him now more than she had that hormone-driven night.

She rubbed her thumb along his lips and heard the catch in his breath.

"I want to kiss you," he said, his voice rough and deep.

Once again she stood at the edge of a cliff, unable to even see what lay below. For the first time in her life, she wanted to jump.

"I'm not stopping you," she said.

Logan pulled her to him and captured her lips in a kiss so gentle and yet so thorough that Skyler's heart opened its door and invited Logan in.

Chapter Fifteen

Logan wrapped his arms around Skyler and pulled her closer. When her hands ran up his back, he deepened the kiss. The feel of her curves, the fruity scent of her assaulted his senses. He could take her here on this couch, wanted to, but she deserved better than that. Better than what he'd given her that night in the hotel. So he broke the kiss.

"Is something wrong?" The worry in Skyler's voice made his heart feel funny, as if it wasn't sure whether to stop beating or pick up the pace.

"No," he said as he caressed her cheek. "Everything's fine."

Doubt passed over her face, and he could feel her pulling away. He cupped the back of her head and planted a soft kiss on her lips. "I don't want to take advantage of you."

"You're the one who's hurt. Maybe I'm the one taking advantage of you."

He leaned back. "Hmm, I might like that."

Her cheeks pinkened, and she lowered her gaze as if she couldn't believe what she'd said. Deciding to give her an out, he said, "I need to get a glass of water. I feel like I swallowed half the arena." He started to stand, but she placed her hand on his leg.

"I'll get it."

He knew she was tired and he wanted to spare her any

extra effort, but he got the sense she needed the space. He let her go but couldn't take his eyes off her.

The moment Skyler had touched his face, something had shifted deep inside Logan. It was a simple gesture and yet it was intimate, more so than anything he'd ever experienced. He'd always hated feeling trapped or confined for too long, but at the moment he wanted nothing more than to stay in this apartment with her until they were both so physically sated that it would take a week to recover.

But it wasn't just physical. He cared about her, and the look of worry on her face at the hospital had stunned him more than his contact with the ground after being thrown from the bull.

When she returned with the water, she also brought a bowl of pretzels and another of strawberries. "Would you like a sandwich? Or I could cook something."

"No." He extended his hand. "I want you to sit down and rest."

She hesitated for a moment before taking his hand and allowing him to guide her to his side. He took a long drink of water before leaning back and wrapping his arm around her shoulders. She stiffened for a moment before relaxing. She grabbed the TV remote from the couch cushion beside her and turned on the television.

It didn't take long for her to start yawning. Without saying anything, he tucked her against his side. Skyler didn't say anything either, but it was enough that she was allowing his touch. That she hadn't protested as she would have not so long ago. He didn't know what was happening with him and his feelings, but for tonight he wasn't going to examine any of it too closely.

He took the remote from her relaxed fingers a moment after she fell asleep. Not wanting to wake her, he gradually lowered the volume on the TV before clicking it off. Free from thoughts of all the reasons why she shouldn't, Skyler snuggled closer to him. He ran his hand over her soft hair. He itched to gather her in his arms and carry her to bed, but he didn't want to disturb her.

But the longer he sat, the more his back began to ache. He thought about his rides for the past couple of months. Fear shot through him that he was losing his touch, that his days of riding were slipping away. What the hell was he going to do after that? He looked at the woman nestled next to him and wondered what part she would play in his life in the months and years ahead. He let himself imagine settling down, getting a job like most normal people. Anxiety knotted his muscles, and he had to force himself not to get up to pace it away.

But the idea of leaving Skyler and their baby behind didn't sit well either. He had to find some sort of compromise, but the more he tried to figure one out, the more his head began to throb. He rested his head against the back of the couch. Gradually his racing thoughts started to slow, eventually to the point where they were hard to form and felt as if they were swimming through molasses. Some new thought tried to take shape but drifted off into nothing as he ceased to think.

"Logan!"

Pain shot through his head as he came awake. He lifted his palm to his forehead as he tried to remember where he was and why his head hurt so damn much. Had he gotten drunk?

"Logan, are you okay?"

He blinked a couple of times and attempted to identify who was talking to him. It clicked as Skyler's face came into focus.

"Say something," she said.

"Why did you wake me up?"

"Because…" She looked at a loss for words. "Aren't you supposed to stay awake?"

He lifted his hand to her face. "Stop worrying. I promise, I'm fine. Nothing worse than a headache."

"You're not just saying that?"

He smiled. "What, and miss the opportunity to have you cater to my every whim?"

She sighed in exasperation. "Are you ever serious?"

One of his typical smartass comments was on his lips, but he didn't let the words form. "When the situation calls for it."

The look on her face told him she didn't believe him. She pulled away and stood. "I'll be right back."

When she returned a couple of minutes later, she held a quilt, sheet and pillow in her arms. He stood and took them from her, then tossed them on the couch.

"I need to make up the couch so you can actually lie down to sleep," she said.

"I don't want to sleep on the couch."

"Oh, okay. I guess it does make more sense for you to sleep in the bed. You're taller, and the couch probably wouldn't be comfortable."

"I don't want you to sleep on the couch either."

Her eyes met his, and her mouth fell open a little. Before she could think of a reason to say no, he closed the space between them and captured her mouth with his. Need consumed him as he pulled her close. She felt so good, so right pressed next to his body, her softness contrasting with his hardness. He broke the kiss and looked down at her.

"If you don't want this, I'll stop. I'll sleep on the couch, or I'll go back to the ranch."

Skyler gripped the front of his shirt. "You're not leaving." She looked up at him, and it was almost as if he could see a storm roiling in her eyes. Her hand slid down his chest, then captured his hand. With a look of yearning that mirrored how he felt, she led him toward her bedroom.

She stopped beside the bed and looked up at him. "I'm scared."

He didn't have to ask why. "I won't hurt you."

Even in the dim light he could see the battle inside her, one side telling her not to trust his words and the other wanting to believe.

She reached up and started unbuttoning his shirt. "Elissa, India and I once had a conversation about which parts of the male body attracted us most. Care to guess what my answer was."

"Smile." As if to illustrate, he smiled at her.

"You do have a nice smile." She finished unbuttoning his shirt and spread it wide, pushing it halfway down his arms. Then she ran her hands up his chest and across his biceps. "But show me a great chest and arms, and I'm a goner."

"Do I measure up?"

This time she smiled. "Oh, yeah."

He sucked in a breath when she lowered her mouth to one of his nipples. He tangled his fingers in her hair and brought her mouth to his.

He wanted to rip all of her clothing off and drive himself into her, but they'd gone the wild-and-crazy route before. He knew her now, cared about her. He couldn't put a name on what he felt, because that would probably freak him the hell out, but Skyler Harrington was definitely more special than that night in the motel would indicate.

So he slowly undressed her, taking his time to kiss every bit of skin he exposed.

"You're killing me here," Skyler breathed as he blazed a slow trail up her neck to her ear.

"Tell me what you want me to do," he said into her ear. He smiled at the shiver he felt go through her body.

"Take off those pants and make love to me."

He stepped back and grinned as he took his time removing his jeans. When they hit the floor and she looked him up and down, his body reacted in a flash. When she licked her lips, she made it damn near impossible to go slow. He swept her up in his arms, ignoring the pain in his back.

When she lay beside him, he caressed her cheek. "You're so beautiful."

"Says the man about to get what he wants."

"If you were dressed in head-to-toe winter-weather gear, you'd still take my breath away."

Surprise flashed in her eyes, and he was a little stunned himself. His words had come from deep within him, from his heart. He was falling for this woman, and falling hard. The fact that he didn't mind was the biggest shock of all.

He placed his hand on her stomach. "I don't want to hurt you or the baby."

Skyler ran her hand over his hip. "You won't."

Even if he didn't hurt her physically, he hoped he could keep his promise of never hurting her emotionally.

He pulled her close and made love to the woman who'd somehow become more important to him than he would have ever thought possible.

Skyler lay on her side watching Logan sleep. The man was gorgeous. Wide shoulders, narrow hips, powerful legs. And his chest and arms—it was all she could do not to run her hands all over him. If she'd thought their first night together had been amazing, it paled in comparison to last night. Maybe it was because this time she hadn't been second-guessing herself. She'd wanted to be with him fully this time, and the last thing she wanted to do this morning was leave him.

After his close call the night before, she wanted to beg him not to ride again. But she didn't have that right. Neither of them had spoken of any kind of commitment other than being there for their child, but as she watched the gentle rise and fall of his chest, she imagined what a life with him might be like. The doubt that he'd ever be able to fully commit to a stable life tugged at her. If he couldn't give up the life of adventure he led, she wouldn't ask him to. But she wouldn't be able to give all of herself to him, not if she didn't want her heart broken over and over again.

But she wasn't going to worry about that today. Now she was going to make him breakfast. And if she was very lucky, she would get the opportunity to let her hands roam all over that awesome body of his again.

She was sliding the French toast and bacon onto plates when Logan wandered out of the bedroom. He'd pulled on his jeans, but thankfully had left his shirt behind.

He walked barefoot toward her, rounding the end of the bar and stopping next to her. "A beautiful woman made me breakfast? I think I might have died last night and gone to heaven."

Her breath caught. "Don't even joke about that."

"Hey," he said, pulling her to him. "I'm okay."

"I know. I'm sorry."

He ran his thumb across her cheek. "Don't apologize. It's nice having someone worry about me."

She caught an odd note in his voice, and it made her think that maybe his untethered lifestyle wasn't as perfect as he told himself. She glanced up at him, and she liked the look of him fresh from bed and standing in her kitchen. She liked it a lot.

She took the plates to the table, and Logan followed, pausing to give her a kiss on the cheek. He slipped into his seat and immediately took a bite of the French toast. He moaned and closed his eyes. "My God, woman, this is delicious."

She smiled at his reaction, and a wave of happiness went through her.

Logan was halfway through eating his breakfast before he came up for air. "I think I might have to keep you here for the foreseeable future. Between your cooking and making love to you, this is paradise."

Heat surged up Skyler's neck to her face.

"Anyone ever tell you that you're even more beautiful when you blush?"

She looked across the table at him. "Anyone ever tell you that it's a crime you ever have to wear a shirt?"

One of his brows shot up, and a naughty smile tugged at his lips. "Is that so?"

By the time they left the bedroom for the second time, the day was half gone, what remained of their breakfast was cold and Skyler had a dozen texts from Elissa and India. Logan walked up behind her as she read the last one. When he started kissing her neck, she tossed the phone aside.

"I should get back to work at the ranch."

She spun in his arms to face him. "Don't go."

He looked down at her with an expression that made her heart expand. She tried not to assign meaning when she wasn't sure, but it gave her hope that maybe they were at the beginning of something that might last.

"I'll stay as long as you want me to."

She was scared to admit that her answer would be forever.

LOGAN STOOD BACK and admired the newly painted ranch house. It looked damned good, if he did say so himself. As he scanned the land around him, he realized he'd hate leaving here. But Skyler needed to sell the place, and he couldn't live here rent-free forever. The thought of getting a place of his own made him twitch a little. He reminded himself that he was in control of his life. He could go or stay as he wished, and the need to stay near Skyler had grown substantially stronger the day before, when they hadn't set foot outside of her apartment. They'd watched a movie, talked some about their families, had a good-natured argument about whether they were having a boy or a girl and spent a good bit of time in bed together. His body strained at the memory, wanting to find that satisfaction again.

He forced himself to return his focus to work. It was a shame Skyler had to sell the ranch. He'd like to see their child running through the yard, learning to ride a horse here, making hay-bale forts in the barn. But he understood why she wanted it gone, and not just because she could use the money to expand her business opportunities in the park. The hurt on her beautiful face when she'd told him about how hard her mother had worked in Skyler's dad's absence, how she'd poured her heart and soul into the ranch, had left him wanting to erase those painful memories for her.

What if he actually could? A crazy idea formed, but it didn't even surprise him. Crazy and unexpected seemed to be riding shotgun with him lately. Maybe erasing bad memories was too much of a stretch, but how about replacing them with good ones? Helping her remember the good times that were no doubt there in her past but overshadowed by the pain.

He hopped in his truck and headed toward town, his plan taking root more firmly with each passing moment. By the time he pulled into the parking lot for Elissa's nursery, there was no going back.

He took a path that meandered through scores of flowerpots and huge planters to reach the front door. Inside was room after room filled with all manner of yard decor, plants and flowers in every color. He finally found Elissa on a ladder hanging wind chimes from the crossbeams.

"Hey, you take a wrong turn somewhere?" she asked.

"You got a minute?"

"Depends. Am I going to like what you're about to say?"

It took him a moment to realize that she must think he was trying to maneuver an escape, that he was trying to use her to shield him from Skyler. Just the thought of doing that knotted his gut.

"I need some landscaping advice."

The surprise on Elissa's face was priceless, but she recovered quickly. "This is for the ranch house?"

"Yeah. Should liven up the place a bit."

She leaned her forearm against one of the ladder's steps. "I already told you you're doing way more than Skyler wanted."

He shrugged. "Just trying to do a good job."

"But you've sunk a lot of money into what you've done, painting the house and now landscaping. Why?"

He quickly ran back over his plan in his mind one more time before speaking. "Because when she sees it, I don't want her to remember anything bad that would hurt her."

Elissa stared at him. "You care about her, don't you?"

"Yes, I do." He didn't even hesitate, because it was as true as anything he'd ever felt.

"Do you love her?"

That feeling of being trapped threatened, but he pushed it away. How should he answer her question? He didn't have a lot of experience with being in love. None, really. "I think I might."

Elissa's smile could have brightened the deepest depths of a cave as she descended the ladder and approached him. She gave him a playful punch in the shoulder. "Then come on. We've got some plant shopping to do."

Over the next few days, Elissa and he handled restoring the flowerbeds around the house and planting several native plants along the fence that paralleled the driveway. Elissa recruited India and her stepdaughter, Ginny, Verona and Lara, the teenage girl who worked in India's store, to help clean the inside of the house. Somehow they were all able to keep what they were doing from reaching Skyler.

"Hey, I don't mind telling a few white lies in the name of the greater good," Elissa said when she got off the phone with Skyler one afternoon.

"You don't think she's suspicious, do you?"

"Nah. You just keep taking her for ice-cream cones and for walks around the lake, and we'll be good."

He did that and more, spending time with Skyler every day. It surprised him how much he began to miss her if he went too long without being able to pull her into his arms and kiss that wonderful mouth of hers. Every day, he thought back to the question Elissa had asked him at the nursery, if he loved Skyler. Though it made him nervous to admit it, he couldn't imagine what else to call what he felt for her.

"It's a shame that someone else will get to enjoy the fruits of our labors," India said the afternoon after she and the others had finished the necessary work inside.

"It's what she wants," Elissa said.

So Skyler said, but he had to wonder if she would feel the same way after he showed her the completed project. He was still wondering about it long after the others had left.

When his phone rang, he expected it to be Skyler. But he didn't recognize the number and almost didn't answer. He needed to go get cleaned up so he could head over to Skyler's.

"Hello?"

"Logan, this is Jimmy Swanson. How ya doing?" Swanson was a retired bull rider who had taught Logan a lot in his early days on the circuit.

"Good. You?"

"Can't complain. Listen, I heard you got injured. Not sure if you're up to riding again yet, but I thought you might like to know that they're having a special riding event up here in Missoula. The Hendersons are going to retire Hot Tamale, but before they do that, they're going to have this event to give everyone one last chance to see if anyone can ride him."

Hot Tamale had never been ridden to the full eight seconds and was going to go down in the history books as one of the toughest bulls to ever be a part of the circuit. He was also the bastard that had thrown Logan at the first rodeo after he'd left Blue Falls following Skyler's baby news. The lure of riding again tugged at him, that need to challenge himself. But he'd given his word to Skyler that she could depend on him.

"There's big money in the pot for anyone who can manage to stay on that mean SOB," Jimmy said.

"What kind of money are we talking?"

Long after the call was over, Logan sat in the gathering dark and thought about his options. His decision made, he headed for the shower.

SKYLER'S HEART RACED at the rap on her door. She wondered if that would ever stop, the excitement when she knew she was only moments away from being in Logan's arms again. She still couldn't believe how happy she felt just thinking about him, let alone actually feeling his touch, breathing in his scent.

As she opened the door, she wondered if she looked as giddy as she felt. "I was beginning to think you'd stood me up."

He stepped inside and pulled her close. "Just worked a little later than normal."

"You've been working so hard, it seems like you've had time to build an entire new house out there."

"Just slow, I guess." He lowered his lips to hers, cutting off further conversation.

She was never going to get tired of this. They hadn't talked about the future beyond what they hoped for the baby, but she was content to go along as they were for now if pressing him for more would only push him away. After opening herself up to the kind of feelings he caused in her, she didn't want to live without them again.

He lifted his lips from hers and framed her face with his strong hands. Her heart stuttered when she saw something in his eyes that hadn't been there before.

"What's wrong?"

"Nothing."

"No, something's different. You look like you're dreading something."

He let his hands slide away from her face to clasp her hands. Nervousness started to build inside her.

"I need to take a trip for a few days."

A wave of panic hit her followed by anger, more at herself than him. She'd known deep down that he wouldn't be able to stay. And she'd let him carve out a part of her heart for himself, just as her mom had with her dad. Skyler wanted to rip her hands away from him, shove him out the door, pretend that he'd never meant anything to her, that they'd never met. But she did none of those things. Well, she did remove her hands from his, but not in the angry way she'd imagined. She took a couple of steps away from him, needing the distance that would only grow when he left. It was important that she take the first step, to not be the victim.

"You're going somewhere to ride."

"Yes, it's a big opportunity. But I'll be back in a few days."

How many times had she heard her father say something similar? She wanted to rail at him the way she'd always wanted her mother to, but she couldn't find the words. It hit her then that maybe her mother had just held her hurt inside, that she hadn't wanted to let Skyler's father know how much his leaving pained her. Skyler knew her mother had been strong, but now she realized just how strong she'd had to be when the man she loved drove away with a piece of her heart.

"Do you think it's wise to get back up on a bull?" She tried to sound like no more than a concerned friend when what she wanted was to plead with him not to put his life at risk again. But she couldn't. She didn't want him to stay unless it was his choice. Keeping him here against his will would only lead to misery for both of them. Like her mother, she would be the strong one.

"It's just one ride."

As she glanced at him, she thought he even believed that. Though her head felt heavy, she nodded. "When do you leave?"

She saw the apology in his eyes before he spoke.

"Tonight. I need to be in Montana day after tomorrow."

Her chest tightened, making it difficult to draw a breath. No matter how wonderful the time they had spent together, she wasn't enough for him. That lure of adventure and the open road was a siren song he couldn't resist no matter how hard he might try.

Logan strode toward her. "I'm coming back, Skyler. I promise you that."

She held up her hand to stop him before he could touch her. If he did, she would shatter. "Please don't make me any promises."

"Why? Because you don't think I'll keep them?"

She forced herself to meet his eyes. "We both knew this day would come. I'm amazed you've been able to stay in one place this long." She felt mean saying the words, but it was all she had as a defense against her heart being irreparably broken.

"That's not fair. Expecting me to never step foot out of Blue Falls again is unreasonable."

"I don't expect that."

Logan's expression tightened, as if she'd wounded him.

"I went into this knowing the kind of man you are, Logan."

"The kind who leaves, right?" He sounded angry now.

"One who doesn't like to be tied down." She lowered her eyes, glancing at her stomach. "I won't keep you from seeing the baby." Somehow she'd make sure her child was happy despite infrequent visits from Logan. She'd love the child enough for both of them.

"Stop it." The anger in Logan's voice drew her gaze back up to his. "I'm not your father. I'm not going to disappear and pop up only whenever I happen to be nearby."

"Okay." She wanted to believe him, wanted it with all her heart and soul, but she only said it so he would leave. The longer he stayed, the more likely she would fall apart in front of him.

He closed the distance between them and gripped her shoulders. "I swear to you I'm coming back."

But when?

As if he'd heard her question, he pulled her close and kissed her as if sealing his promise. She should have pushed him away, but she didn't have the strength. She needed to feel him one more time before he walked out that door, so she held him tightly and kissed him with all the love she felt for him.

When he broke the kiss, Logan whispered against her lips. "Please believe me, Skyler."

She nodded. He kissed her again, then held her close, her cheek against that chest that was a constant star in her dreams of him. She listened to the steady rhythm of his heartbeat and wished she could have him hold her like this forever.

Eventually, however, he eased away from her. "I need to go."

She didn't say anything, not trusting her voice as she allowed him to lead her to the door. Logan dropped another kiss on her lips, this one soft and lingering, before he stepped out the door. Unwilling to watch him walk away from her for possibly the last time, she closed the door and leaned her cheek and palm against it. When she heard his truck start, the tears pooled in her eyes broke free.

Chapter Sixteen

Skyler blamed fatigue for staying in bed the next morning, begging off a planned breakfast with Elissa and India. But her friends knew her too well and showed up at her apartment. She ignored them when they knocked and called out to her, hoping they'd go away and leave her alone. She felt wretched, and after a night of crying she was sure she looked it, too.

"Skyler, we're not going away, so open the door," Elissa said.

She managed to drag herself out of bed. Might as well get this conversation over with. It had to be better than listening to Elissa bang on her door all day, which she certainly would.

The moment she opened the door, she saw the shock on their faces.

"Sky, what's wrong?" India stepped inside and grabbed Skyler's hands.

"Logan's gone."

"Gone? What do you mean?"

"He left for Montana last night, back to the rodeo circuit."

"That doesn't make any sense." Elissa looked confused.

"Of course it does. We all knew this would happen eventually. I just fooled myself for a little while that maybe he'd changed."

"He did," Elissa insisted with some sort of meaningful glance at India.

"Obviously not."

"What did he say?" India asked.

"Oh, that he'd be back in a few days. Seems I've heard that before."

"I believe him," Elissa said. "You should, too."

Skyler bit her lip against a sudden tremble. "I want to. You can't know how much I want to."

"Go get dressed. There's something you need to see."

"I don't feel like going anywhere."

India squeezed her hand gently. "Elissa's right. It'll be good for you to get out, anyway. Staying cooped up in here crying isn't good for you or the baby."

If it had just been her, Skyler would have pushed her friends out the door and spent the day any way she pleased, probably with a giant self-pity party that involved ice cream and a movie marathon where women kicked guys' asses. But at the mention of her baby's welfare, she took a deep breath and turned toward her bedroom.

After she was showered and dressed, she allowed her friends to drive her away from the inn on some mysterious mission. Her heart ached when she remembered the last time they'd done something like this, the day she'd met Logan, just before he'd jumped out of a plane with her.

When she realized they were headed to the ranch, she stiffened. She didn't want to go there, for so many reasons. "Why are we going to the ranch? I told you, he's gone."

"Because you need to see why we believe he's coming back."

Her breath caught when they came within view of the ranch. Logan had repainted the house. Gone was the weathered exterior, replaced by bright new white paint with black trim and door. As Elissa turned into the driveway, Skyler noticed the plants along the edge of the freshly painted fence. No wonder he'd spent so much time out here. How much had he spent on a home that wasn't even his? That would someday belong to a stranger.

When Elissa parked, Skyler couldn't move at first. "I had no idea he'd done so much."

"You haven't even seen the inside," India said.

There was more? Her heart sped up as she noticed all the new flowers and shrubs that filled her mother's old flowerbeds. The rotted timbers around the beds had been replaced with new ones. She climbed the steps and used her second key to open the front door. The smell of new paint hit her as she stepped into a house that didn't look as if it had been abandoned. It felt new and alive. She walked from room to room, looking at the bright colors and how clean everything was.

When she got to her old bedroom, the new coat of purple paint caused tears to blur her vision. She spun in a slow circle. "How? Why?"

Elissa leaned on the doorframe. "He may have had some help."

Skyler looked from Elissa to India and back. "You all helped him?"

"Among others," Elissa said.

"Why?"

"Because he asked us to."

Skyler shook her head. "I don't understand."

"It's not that hard to figure out. That man loves you."

"That can't be it."

"Why? Because he hasn't said it? He's a dude. It's easier for them to paint a house than say those three little words."

India crossed the room to stand beside Skyler. "You should have seen him here, Sky. He looked like a man on a mission."

Skyler sank onto the edge of her childhood bed and thought she caught a whiff of Logan's scent. If she were alone, she'd curl up in the bed and inhale deeply until she filled herself with the part of him that lingered.

"He'll be back," Elissa said, conviction in her voice. "And

if he doesn't show up, I will hunt him down and make him wish he'd never set foot in Texas, let alone Blue Falls."

Skyler laughed, a miracle considering how incredibly alone and hollowed out she'd felt since the night before. As she sat in the house that had for so long held only painful memories for her, a spark of hope lit inside her and began to grow. She just prayed that the things she'd said to him the night before hadn't made Logan change his mind about coming back.

"ARE YOU SURE about this?"

Logan looked at his mother, who sat in the same chair he'd seen her sit in nearly his entire life. "Yes, positive."

After successfully riding Hot Tamale and collecting his impressive winnings, he'd made another decision. So he'd hit the road again, this time for North Dakota to see his family and to sell out his portion of the family ranch to his brothers and sister.

"So you're really never coming back here?"

"I'll come for visits, but there's somewhere else I've got to be." He took a deep breath before continuing. "There's someone I care about in Texas, and we're going to have a child."

His mother's eyes widened as sounds of surprise filled the room.

"Are you going to marry her?" His father sounded as if he already knew the answer and didn't like it.

Instead of getting angry, Logan met his father's eyes and smiled. "If she'll have me."

Andrea, his younger sister, crossed the room and gathered him in her arms. "I'm so happy for you."

He hugged her back and realized how much he'd missed his family. He'd never consciously thought about it, because thoughts of them were always so tangled up with their inability to understand the way he chose to live his life.

"Will you still ride?" Eric, his oldest brother, asked.

"I think my days of riding bulls are over." If he'd needed an exclamation point on that decision, it had been how he'd felt the morning after riding Hot Tamale—as though he'd been body-slammed for about an hour straight. He'd lost count of how many curse words he'd used just trying to get out of bed the next morning.

By midafternoon all the paperwork was done and he had a substantial check in hand. As he walked toward his truck, his mother caught up to him. "Next time you come for a visit, bring your Skyler and the baby, okay?"

He nodded.

"And…when the baby comes, I'd like to come visit you if that's okay."

He wouldn't have been more surprised if a flying saucer full of little green men had landed next to them. "I'd like that. I think you would enjoy visiting Blue Falls."

She smiled up at him and placed her palm against his cheek. "I'm sorry we've been so hard on you. For me it was worry. I was so afraid you'd get hurt far from home. But by holding you too tightly, I just pushed you away. We all did."

A huge chunk of the resentment toward his family slid away. Maybe it was because he was about to become a father and he knew he'd do anything to keep his child safe. He leaned forward and kissed his mom on her forehead. "It's in the past. No sense hanging on to it."

As he hit the road back toward Texas, he hoped he could convince Skyler of the same thing.

SKYLER WALKED BACK to her office after consulting with Amelia about a group scheduled to arrive later that afternoon. She glanced at her apartment door adjacent to her office and couldn't help remembering the night Logan had kissed her there. With each passing day, she grew more anxious that he was gone for good, despite Elissa's and India's confidence that he would be back.

As soon as she sat down behind her desk, the phone rang.

"Skyler Harrington," she answered.

"Hey, Skyler. It's Justine. I've got good news for you. We've finally got a buyer for your ranch."

Pain blossomed in her chest. After all the years of wanting to be rid of the ranch, now the thought of letting it go broke her heart. Since the day she'd seen all the work Logan had put into it, she'd started focusing on the good memories from her childhood. Her mom pushing her on the swing in the backyard. Her dad holding her hand as she walked barefoot along the top of the fence. She couldn't have been more than four or five, and she'd felt as if she was the queen of the world. It felt wrong to let it go to strangers who wouldn't have those memories, who wouldn't know how much what Logan had done meant to her.

But it didn't make financial sense to keep a place she didn't use.

"Skyler?"

"Yeah, I'm here."

"The buyer is ready to begin the paperwork today but would like to meet you and talk about some aspects of the ranch I don't know about. Can you meet us out there in an hour?"

No, this was moving too fast. Would the ranch be gone before she even got to thank Logan for all the work he did to make this possible?

"Uh, yeah."

As she drove out to the ranch, her heart ached. But with the funds she'd get from this sale, she'd be able to complete the additions to the park, things that everyone could enjoy and would hopefully bring more tourists to town. That would help all the businesses, not just hers.

Justine waved to her as Skyler got out of her car.

"Hey, perfect timing. We've only been here a couple of minutes."

Curious who might be calling the ranch home soon, she followed Justine into the house and toward the kitchen. When she stepped inside the room where her mother had served many meals, she gasped. Logan stood at the other end of the table watching her. He looked so good that she wanted to run into his arms, but she almost didn't trust her eyes. Was he really there?

She glanced toward Justine, but she'd slipped out of the room. She shifted her gaze back toward Logan, half expecting him to have disappeared, as well. "Why are you here?"

"I told you I'd come back."

"But why the ruse to get me to come out here? You could have stopped by the inn."

"Because you need a buyer for the ranch, and I'm prepared to buy it from you."

She tilted her head, not sure if she'd heard him correctly. "Why would you buy the ranch?"

"Because I need somewhere to live."

She shook her head, still not clear on what was going on. "I don't understand. I said you could stay here."

"In exchange for working on the place. The work is done."

"Wouldn't an apartment make more sense?"

He rounded the table and walked slowly toward her. "No. I'm pretty sure they wouldn't want bulls in the yard."

"What?"

He stopped so close to her that she could reach out and touch him if she allowed herself. "I've ridden in my last rodeo, but I'm going to raise bulls for the rodeo circuit. I need a place to do that. I need a home."

Skyler's heart rate increased even more at the thought that he might really and truly be staying for good. That she'd be able to see him and their child would grow up knowing his or her father.

"Before anyone signs on any dotted lines, though, I need to ask you something."

"Okay."

"Would you ever consider living here with me?"

Skyler gripped the back of a chair for support as Logan pulled something from his pocket.

"I'm willing to buy the ranch, but I'd rather you keep it and we make a life here together. You, me and our child." He lifted a little black box and popped it open.

The diamond-and-amethyst ring inside took her breath away. She met Logan's eyes. "What…" She swallowed against the lump in her throat and tried again. "What does this mean?"

She saw understanding in those beautiful eyes of his.

"It means I love you, Skyler Harrington, and I want you to be my wife. It means that I'm never going to abandon you or our baby. It means that I want to make a life here with you, if you'll have me."

She lifted a shaking hand and placed it against his jaw. "Are you sure that's what you want? You're not just doing this because you think it's what I want you to say?"

He smiled. "Does that mean you want to marry me?"

"Answer my question first."

"I've never been more sure of anything in my life. The entire time I was away, all I could think about was how fast I could get back here and hold you in my arms again. And no, I never thought I'd ever say something quite so corny."

Skyler smiled, and joy burst to brilliant life within her. "I like corny. And I love you, more than I ever thought myself capable of." She pressed herself against him and captured his lips with hers.

Logan kissed her so deeply that she felt his love for her all the way to her toes. When they finally came up for air, Logan laughed. "I'm going to take a wild guess that that was a yes to my proposal."

"Good guess," she said, then kissed him again.

Skyler didn't know how long they stood in the kitchen kissing, but by the time they wandered hand in hand out to the porch Justine was already gone.

"I guess she figured out her services weren't needed," Logan said.

"And I'd wager it won't be long before half of Blue Falls knows why." Skyler laughed. "Verona is going to be impossible after this. She's two for two this summer."

"Elissa better watch out."

That made Skyler laugh even more. "It'll serve her right."

Logan pulled Skyler close and dropped little kisses along her cheek. "I happen to like the fact that your friends are matchmakers."

"Me, too." She ran her hands up his chest. "You know, I seem to remember saying something about it being a crime for you to wear shirts."

"You plan to report me to the police?"

"No, I have a better idea." She tugged the bottom of the T-shirt out of his jeans and slid her hands over his heated flesh before she started walking backward toward the front door.

Logan gave her that mischievous smile she'd come to love. "I like how you think, woman."

She did, too, because she was thinking that life couldn't get more perfect.

* * * * *

*Be sure to look for Trish Milburn's next book
in her BLUE FALLS, TEXAS miniseries!
Available in 2014 wherever Harlequin books are sold.*

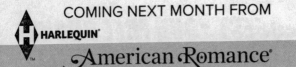

COMING NEXT MONTH FROM
HARLEQUIN
American Romance

Available October 1, 2013

#1469 TWINS UNDER THE CHRISTMAS TREE
The Cash Brothers • by Marin Thomas

Conway Cash is ready to settle down with a good woman, but he's dead set against being a dad. So why does his blood boil when his single-mom pal Isi Lopez starts dating someone else?

#1470 BIG SKY CHRISTMAS
Coffee Creek, Montana • by C.J. Carmichael

Jackson Stone shouldn't be attracted to Winnie Hayes. After all, he was responsible for her fiancé's death. But he has a chance at redemption—and to be the man Winnie and her son need.

#1471 HER WYOMING HERO
Daddy Dude Ranch • by Rebecca Winters

Kathryn Wentworth will do anything to protect her son. Can she count on help from Ross Livingston to escape her old life and start a new one—with him?

#1472 A RANCHER'S CHRISTMAS
Saddlers Prairie • by Ann Roth

Gina Arnett wants to sell the ranch she recently inherited, but she's unprepared for the persuasive ways of ranch manager Zach Horton, who made a promise to do everything in his power to convince her to keep it.

REQUEST YOUR FREE BOOKS!
2 FREE NOVELS PLUS 2 FREE GIFTS!

⬦ HARLEQUIN™

American ★ Romance®

LOVE, HOME & HAPPINESS

YES! Please send me 2 FREE Harlequin® American Romance® novels and my 2 FREE gifts (gifts are worth about $10). After receiving them, if I don't wish to receive any more books, I can return the shipping statement marked "cancel." If I don't cancel, I will receive 4 brand-new novels every month and be billed just $4.74 per book in the U.S. or $5.24 per book in Canada. That's a savings of at least 14% off the cover price! It's quite a bargain! Shipping and handling is just 50¢ per book in the U.S. and 75¢ per book in Canada.* I understand that accepting the 2 free books and gifts places me under no obligation to buy anything. I can always return a shipment and cancel at any time. Even if I never buy another book, the two free books and gifts are mine to keep forever.

154/354 HDN F4YN

Name	(PLEASE PRINT)	

Address		Apt. #

City	State/Prov.	Zip/Postal Code

Signature (if under 18, a parent or guardian must sign)

Mail to the **Harlequin**® Reader Service:
IN U.S.A.: P.O. Box 1867, Buffalo, NY 14240-1867
IN CANADA: P.O. Box 609, Fort Erie, Ontario L2A 5X3

Want to try two free books from another line?
Call 1-800-873-8635 or visit www.ReaderService.com.

* Terms and prices subject to change without notice. Prices do not include applicable taxes. Sales tax applicable in N.Y. Canadian residents will be charged applicable taxes. Offer not valid in Quebec. This offer is limited to one order per household. Not valid for current subscribers to Harlequin American Romance books. All orders subject to credit approval. Credit or debit balances in a customer's account(s) may be offset by any other outstanding balance owed by or to the customer. Please allow 4 to 6 weeks for delivery. Offer available while quantities last.

Your Privacy—The Harlequin® Reader Service is committed to protecting your privacy. Our Privacy Policy is available online at www.ReaderService.com or upon request from the Harlequin Reader Service.

We make a portion of our mailing list available to reputable third parties that offer products we believe may interest you. If you prefer that we not exchange your name with third parties, or if you wish to clarify or modify your communication preferences, please visit us at www.ReaderService.com/consumerschoice or write to us at Harlequin Reader Service Preference Service, P.O. Box 9062, Buffalo, NY 14269. Include your complete name and address.

HAR13R

SPECIAL EXCERPT FROM

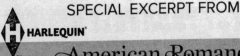

HARLEQUIN
American Romance

*Meet the Cash Brothers—six hunky cowboys
with charm to spare!
Read on for a special excerpt from*
TWINS UNDER THE CHRISTMAS TREE
*by Marin Thomas
Available October 2013*

A sixth sense told Conway he was being watched. He opened his eyes beneath the cowboy hat covering his face. Two pairs of small athletic shoes stood side by side next to the sofa.

"Is he dead?"

"Poke him and see," whispered a second voice.

Conway shifted on the couch and groaned.

"He's alive."

"Maybe he's sick."

"Look under his hat."

"You look."

Conway's chest shook with laughter. Small fingers lifted the brim of his hat and suddenly Conway's gaze clashed with the boys'. They shrieked and jumped back.

He pointed to one kid. "What's your name?"

"Javier."

Conway moved his finger to the other boy.

"I'm Miguel. Who are you?"

"Conway Cash."

Javier whispered in his brother's ear, then Miguel asked, "Why are you sleeping on our couch?"

"Your mom wasn't feeling well, so I stayed the night."

"Javi…Mig…. Where are you guys?" Isi's sluggish voice rang out a moment before she appeared in the hallway.

"Mom, Conway Cash slept on our couch."

"It was nice of Mr. Conway to stay, but I'm fine now." Isi sent him a time-to-leave look.

Conway stood and handed her a piece of paper. "Your sitter left this for you last night. She wanted you to read it first thing in the morning."

While Isi read the note, Conway said, "I'd really like to make it up to you for what happened last night. Is there anything I can—"

Isi glanced up from the note, a stunned expression on her face.

"What's wrong?" he asked.

"Nicole quit. She's moving to Tucson to live with her father."

"Maybe your mother could help out with the boys."

"I told you a long time ago that I don't have any family. It's just me and the boys." She paused. "You offered to help. Would you watch the boys until I find a replacement sitter?"

Babysit? Him? "I don't think that's a good idea."

"It would be for two or three days at the most."

"I don't know anything about kids."

"Never mind." Her shoulders sagged.

Oh, hell. How hard could it be to watch a couple of four-year-olds? "Okay, I'll watch them."

She flashed him a bright smile. "You'll need to be here by noon on Monday."

"See you then." Right now, Conway couldn't escape fast enough.

Find out if Conway survives his new babysitting duties in
TWINS UNDER THE CHRISTMAS TREE
by Marin Thomas
Available October 1, 2013, only from
Harlequin® American Romance®.

HARLEQUIN®

American Romance®

A rancher comes to her rescue.

At the magnificent Wyoming dude ranch run by
Ross Livingston and two fellow ex-marines, families
of fallen soldiers find hope and healing. When lovely
widow Kit Wentworth and her son arrive, Ross
immediately finds himself drawn to them. Soon he's
able to bring young Andy out of his shell—and touch
Kit's heart as no other man has.

Her Wyoming Hero
by REBECCA WINTERS

Available October 1, 2013, only from
Harlequin® American Romance®.

HAR75475

A Holiday Change of Heart

Gina Arnett comes home to Saddlers Prairie to say goodbye to her uncle and sell the family ranch she's just inherited. Her focus is on getting back to Chicago and her high-powered job. Two things change her plans: a sudden blizzard that causes the town to be snowed in, and Zach Horton—the ranch foreman who tries to convince her to stay. He's not the kind of man she dreamed of falling for. But at Christmas, all dreams seem possible....

A Rancher's Christmas

by ANN ROTH

Available October 1, 2013, only from Harlequin® American Romance®.